PUFFIN BOOKS

MARY POPPINS IN THE PARK

Hot summer days with Mary Poppins in the Park hold many magical surprises for Michael and Jane. They meet a lonely lion looking for his policeman, Michael has a strange adventure in a world ruled by cats, Jane meets some tiny people and everybody has an unforgettable Hallowe'en! And through all the excitement sails the calm and unforgettable Mary Poppins, the best nanny anyone ever had.

These enduringly popular stories are now published in Puffins, together with *Mary Poppins, Mary Poppins Opens the Door, Mary Poppins in Cherry Tree Lane,* and *Mary Poppins Comes Back.*

P. L. Travers

MARY POPPINS
IN THE PARK

WITH ILLUSTRATIONS BY
MARY SHEPARD

PUFFIN BOOKS

Puffin Books, Penguin Books Ltd, Harmondsworth, Middlesex, England
Viking Penguin Inc., 40 West 23rd Street, New York, New York 10010, U.S.A.
Penguin Books Australia Ltd, Ringwood, Victoria, Australia
Penguin Books Canada Ltd, 2801 John Street, Markham, Ontario, Canada L3R 1B4

First published by Peter Davies 1952
Published in Puffin Books 1984
Reprinted 1985

Copyright 1952 by P. L. Travers
Illustrations copyright 1952 by Mary Shepard
All rights reserved

Made and printed in Great Britain by
Richard Clay (The Chaucer Press) Ltd,
Bungay, Suffolk
Filmset in Monophoto Plantin

The adventures in this book should be understood to have happened during any of the three visits of Mary Poppins to the Banks Family. This is a word of warning to anybody who may be expecting they are in for a fourth visit. She cannot forever arrive and depart. And, apart from that, it should be remembered that three is a lucky number.

Those who already know Mary Poppins will also be familiar with many of the other characters who appear here. And those who don't – if they want to know them more intimately – can find them in the earlier volumes.

P. L. T.

Contents

CHAPTER ONE

Every Goose a Swan

The summer day was hot and still. The cherry-trees that bordered the Lane could feel their cherries ripening – the green slowly turning to yellow and the yellow blushing red.

The houses dozed in the dusty gardens with their shutters over their eyes. 'Do not disturb us!' they seemed to say. 'We rest in the afternoon.'

And the starlings hid themselves in the chimneys with their heads under their wings.

Over the Park lay a cloud of sunlight as thick and as golden as syrup. No wind stirred the heavy leaves. The flowers stood up, very still and shiny, as though they were made of metal.

Down by the Lake the benches were empty. The people who usually sat there had gone home out of the heat. Neleus, the little marble statue, looked down at the placid water. No goldfish flirted a scarlet tail. They were all sitting under the lily-leaves – using them as umbrellas.

The lawns spread out like a green carpet, motionless in the sunlight. Except for a single, rhythmic movement, you might have thought that the whole Park was only a painted picture. To and fro, by the big magnolia, the Park Keeper was spearing up rubbish and putting it into a litter-basket.

He stopped his work and looked up as two dogs trotted by.

They had come from Cherry Tree Lane, he knew,

Sitting bolt upright against the tree

for Miss Lark was calling from behind her shutters.

'Andrew! Willoughby! Please come back! Don't go swimming in that dirty Lake! I'll make you some Iced Tea!'

Andrew and Willoughby looked at each other, winked, and trotted on. But as they passed the big magnolia, they started and pulled up sharply. Down they flopped on the grass, panting – with their pink tongues lolling out.

Mary Poppins, neat and prim in her blue skirt and a new hat trimmed with a crimson tulip, looked at them over her knitting. She was sitting bolt upright against the tree, with a plaid rug spread on the lawn around her. Her handbag sat tidily by her side. And above her, from a flowering branch, the parrot umbrella dangled.

She glanced at the two thumping tails and gave a little sniff.

'Put in your tongues and sit up straight! You are not a pair of wolves.'

The two dogs sprang at once to attention. And Jane, lying on the lawn, could see they were doing their very best to put their tongues in their cheeks.

'And remember, if you're going swimming,' Mary Poppins continued, 'to shake yourselves when you come out. Don't come sprinkling *us*!'

Andrew and Willoughby looked reproachful.

'As though, Mary Poppins,' they seemed to say, 'we would dream of such a thing!'

'All right, then. Be off with you!' And they sped away like shots from a gun.

'Come back!' Miss Lark cried anxiously.

But nobody took any notice.

'Why can't *I* swim in the Park Lake?' asked Michael in a smothered voice. He was lying face downwards in the grass watching a family of ants.

'You're not a dog!' Mary Poppins reminded him.

'I know, Mary Poppins. But if I were –' Was she smiling or not? – he couldn't be sure, with his nose pressed into the earth.

'Well – what would you do?' she inquired, with a sniff.

He wanted to say that if *he* were a dog he would do just as he liked – swim or not, as the mood took him, without asking leave of anyone. But what if her face was looking fierce! Silence was best, he decided.

'Nothing!' he said, in a meek voice. 'It's too hot to argue, Mary Poppins!'

'Out of nothing comes nothing!' She tossed her head in its tulip hat. 'And I'm not arguing, I'm talking!' She was having the last word, as usual.

The sunlight caught her knitting-needles as it shone through the broad magnolia leaves on the little group below. John and Barbara, leaning their heads on each other's shoulders, were dozing and waking, waking and dozing. Annabel was fast asleep in Mary Poppins' shadow. Light and darkness dappled them all and splotched the face of the Park Keeper as he dived at a piece of newspaper.

'All litter to be placed in the baskets! Obey the rules!' he said sternly.

Mary Poppins looked him up and down. Her glance would have withered an oak-tree.

'That's not my litter,' she retorted.

'Oh?' he said disbelievingly.

'No!' she replied, with a virtuous snort.

'Well, *someone* must 'ave put it there. It doesn't grow – like roses!'

He pushed his cap to the back of his head and mopped behind his ears. What with the heat, and her tone of voice, he was feeling quite depressed.

''Ot weather we're 'avin'!' he remarked, eyeing her nervously. He looked like an eager, lonely dog.

'That's what we expect in the middle of summer!' Her knitting-needles clicked.

The Park Keeper sighed and tried again.

'I see you brought yer parrot!' he said, glancing up at the black silk shape that hung among the leaves.

'You mean my *parrot-headed umbrella*,' she haughtily corrected him.

He gave a little anxious laugh. 'You don't think it's goin' to rain, do you? With all this sun about?'

'I don't think, I *know*,' she told him calmly. 'And if I,' she went on, 'were a Park Keeper, I wouldn't be wasting half the day like *some* people I could mention! There's a piece of orange peel over there – why don't you pick it up?'

She pointed with her knitting-needle and kept it pointed accusingly while he speared up the offending litter and tossed it into a basket.

'If *she* was me,' he said to himself, 'there'd be no Park at all. Only a nice tidy desert!' He fanned his face with his cap.

'And anyway,' he said aloud, 'it's no fault of mine I'm a Park Keeper. I should 'ave been a Nexplorer by rights, away in foreign parts. If I'd 'ad me way I wouldn't be 'ere. I'd be sittin' on a piece of ice along with a Polar Bear!'

He sighed and leaned upon his stick, falling into a day-dream.

'Humph!' said Mary Poppins loudly. And a startled dove in the tree above her ruffled its wing in surprise.

A feather came slowly drifting down. Jane stretched out her hand and caught it.

'How deliciously it tickles!' she murmured, running the grey edge over her nose. Then she tucked the feather above her brow and bound her ribbon round it.

'I'm the daughter of an Indian Chief. Minnehaha, Laughing Water, gliding along the river.'

'Oh, no, you're not,' contradicted Michael. 'You're Jane Caroline Banks.'

'That's only my outside,' she insisted. 'Inside I'm somebody quite different. It's a very funny feeling.'

'You should have eaten a bigger lunch. Then you wouldn't have funny feelings. And Daddy's not an Indian Chief, so you can't be Minnehaha!'

He gave a sudden start as he spoke and peered more closely into the grass.

'There he goes!' he shouted wildly, wriggling forward on his stomach and thumping with his toes.

'I'll thank you, Michael,' said Mary Poppins, 'to stop kicking my shins. What are you – a Performing Horse?'

14

'Not a horse, a hunter, Mary Poppins! I'm tracking in the jungle!'

'Jungles!' scoffed the Park Keeper. 'My vote is for snowy wastes!'

'If you're not careful, Michael Banks, you'll be tracking home to bed. I never knew such a silly pair. And you're the third,' snapped Mary Poppins, eyeing the Park Keeper. 'Always wanting to be something else instead of what you are. If it's not Miss Minnie-what's-her-name, it's this or that or the other. You're as bad as the Goose-girl and the Swineherd!'

'But it isn't geese or swine I'm after. It's a lion, Mary Poppins. He may be only an ant on the outside but inside – ah, at last, I've got him! – inside he's a man-eater!'

Michael rolled over, red in the face, holding something small and black between his finger and thumb.

'Jane,' he began in an eager voice. But the sentence was never finished. For Jane was making signs to him, and as he turned to Mary Poppins he understood their meaning.

Her knitting had fallen on to the rug and her hands lay folded in her lap. She was looking at something far away, beyond the Lane, beyond the Park, perhaps beyond the horizon.

Carefully, so as not to disturb her, the children crept to her side. The Park Keeper plumped himself down on the rug and stared at her, goggle-eyed.

'Yes, Mary Poppins?' prompted Jane. 'The Goose-girl – tell us about her!'

Michael pressed against her skirt and waited expectantly. He could feel her legs, bony and strong, beneath the cool blue linen.

From under the shadow of her hat she glanced at them for a short moment, and looked away again.

'Well, there she sat –' she began gravely, speaking in the soft accents that were so unlike her usual voice.

'There she sat, day after day, amid her flock of geese, braiding her hair and unbraiding it for lack of something to do. Sometimes she would pick a fern and wave it before her like a fan, the way the Lord Chancellor's wife might do, or even the Queen, maybe.

'Or again, she would weave a necklace of flowers and go to the brook to admire it. And every time she did that she noticed that her eyes were blue – bluer than any periwinkle – and her cheeks like the breast of the robin. As for her mouth – not to mention her nose! – her opinion of these was so high she had no words fit to describe them.'

'She sounds like you, Mary Poppins,' said Michael. 'So terribly pleased with herself!'

Her glance came darting from the horizon and flickered at him fiercely.

'I mean, Mary Poppins –' he began to stammer. Had he broken the thread of the story?

'I mean,' he went on flatteringly, '*you've* got pink cheeks and blue eyes, too. Like lollipops and bluebells.'

A slow smile of satisfaction melted her angry look, and Michael gave a sigh of relief as she took up the tale again.

Well, she went on, there was the brook, and there was the Goose-girl's reflection. And each time she looked at it she was sorry for everyone in the world who was missing such a spectacle. And she pitied in particular the handsome Swineherd who herded his flock on the other side of the stream.

'If only,' she thought, lamentingly, 'I were not the person I am! If I were merely what I seem, I could then invite him over. But since I am something more than a goose-girl, it would not be right or proper.'

And reluctantly she turned her back and looked in the other direction.

She would have been surprised, perhaps, had she known what the Swineherd was thinking.

He, too, for lack of a looking-glass, made use of the little river. And when it reflected his dark curls, and the curve of his chin and his well-shaped ears, he grieved for the whole human race, thinking of all it was missing. And especially he grieved for the Goose-girl.

'Undoubtedly,' he told himself, 'she is dying of loneliness – sitting there in her shabby dress, braiding her yellow hair. It is very pretty hair, too, and – but for the fact that I am *who* I am – I would willingly speak a word to her and while away the time.'

And reluctantly he turned his back and looked in the other direction.

What a coincidence, you will say! But there's more to the story than that. Not only the Goose-girl and the

Swineherd, but every creature in that place was thinking the same thoughts.

The geese, as they nibbled the buttercups and flattened the grass into star-like shapes, were convinced – and they made no secret of it – they were something more than geese.

And the swine would have laughed at any suggestion that they were merely pigs.

And so it was with the grey Ass who pulled the Swineherd's cart to market; and the Toad who lived beside the stream, under one of the stepping-stones; and the barefoot Boy with the Toy Monkey who played on the bridge every day.

Each believed that his real self was infinitely greater and grander than the one to be seen with the naked eye.

Around his little shaggy body, the Ass was confident, a lordlier, finer, sleeker shape kicked its hooves in the daisies.

To the Toad, however, *his* true self was smaller than his outward shape, and very gay and green. He would gaze for hours at his reflection but, ugly as it truly was, the sight never depressed him.

'That's only my outside,' he would say, nodding at his wrinkled skin and yellow bulging eyes. But he kept his outside out of sight when the Boy was on the bridge. For he dreaded the curses that greeted him if he showed as much as a toe.

'Heave to!' the ferocious voice would cry. 'Enemy sighted to starboard! A bottle of rum and a new dagger to the man who rips him apart!'

For the Boy was something more than a boy – as you'll probably have guessed. Inside, he knew the Straits of Magellan as you know the nose on your face. Honest mariners paled at his fame, his deeds were a byword in seven seas. He could sack a dozen ships in a morning and bury the treasure so cleverly that even he could not find it.

To a passer-by it might have seemed that the Boy had two good eyes. But in his own private opinion, he was only possessed of one. He had lost the other in a hand-to-hand fight somewhere off Gibraltar. His everyday name always made him smile when people called him by it. 'If they knew who I really am,' he would say, 'they wouldn't look so cheerful!'

As for the Monkey, *he* believed he was nothing like a monkey.

'This old fur coat,' he assured himself, 'is simply to keep me warm. And I swing by my tail for the fun of it, not because I must.'

Well, there they all were, one afternoon, full of their fine ideas. The sun spread over them like a fan, very warm and cosy. The meadow flowers hung on their stems, bright as newly-washed china. Up in the sky the larks were singing – on and on, song without end, as though they were all wound up.

The Goose-girl sat among her geese, the Swineherd with his swine. The Ass in his field, and the Toad in his hole, were nodding sleepily. And the Boy and his Monkey lolled on the bridge discussing their further plans for bloodshed.

Suddenly the Ass snorted and his ear gave a questioning twitch. Larks were above and the brook beneath, but he heard among these daily sounds the echo of a footstep.

Along the path that led to the stream a ragged man was lounging. His tattered clothes were so old that you couldn't find one bit of them that wasn't tied with string. The brim of his hat framed a face that was rosy and mild in the sunlight, and through the brim his hair stuck up in tufts of grey and silver. His steps were alternately light and heavy, for one foot wore an old boot and the other a bedroom slipper. You would have to look for a long time to find a shabbier man.

But his shabbiness seemed not to trouble him – indeed, he appeared to enjoy it. For he wandered along contentedly, eating a crust and a pickled onion and whistling between mouthfuls. Then he spied the group in the meadow, and stared, and his tune broke off in the middle.

'A beautiful day!' he said politely, plucking the hatbrim from his head and bowing to the Goose-girl.

She gave him a haughty, tossing glance, but the Tramp did not seem to notice it.

'You two been quarrelling?' he asked, jerking his head at the Swineherd.

The Goose-girl laughed indignantly. 'Quarrelling? What a silly remark! Why, I do not even know him!'

'Well,' said the Tramp, with a cheerful smile, 'would you like me to introduce you?'

'Certainly not!' She flung up her head. 'How could I associate with a Swineherd? I'm a princess in disguise.'

'Indeed?' said the Tramp, looking very surprised. 'If that is the case, I must not detain you. I expect you want to be back at the Palace, getting on with your work.'

'Work? What work?' The Goose-girl stared.

It was now her turn to look surprised. Surely princesses sat upon cushions, with slaves to perform their least command.

'Why, spinning and weaving. And etiquette! Practising patience and cheerfulness while unsuitable suitors beg for your hand. Trying to look as if you liked it when you hear, for the hundred-thousandth time, the King's three silly riddles! Not many princesses – as you must know – have leisure to sit all day in the sun among a handful of geese!'

'But what about wearing a pearly crown? And dancing till dawn with the Sultan's son?'

'Dancing? Pearls? Oh, my! Oh, my!' A burst of laughter broke from the Tramp, as he took from his sleeve a piece of sausage.

'Those crowns are as heavy as lead or iron. You'd have a ridge in your head in no time. And a princess's duty – surely you know? – is to dance with her father's old friends first. Then the Lord Chamberlain. Then the Lord Chancellor. And, of course, the Keeper of the Seal. By the time you get round to the Sultan's son, it's late and he's had to go home.'

The Goose-girl pondered the Tramp's words. Could he really be speaking the truth? All the goose-girls in all the stories were princesses  in disguise. But oh, how difficult it sounded! What did one say to Lord Chamberlains? 'Come here!' 'Go there!' as one would to a goose? Spinning and weaving! Etiquette!

Perhaps, taking everything into account, it might be better, the Goose-girl thought, simply to be a goose-girl.

'Well, away to the Palace!' the Tramp advised her. 'You're wasting your time sitting here, you know! Don't you agree?' he called to the Swineherd, who was listening from his side of the stream.

'Agree with what?' said the Swineherd quickly, as though he hadn't heard a word. 'I never concern myself with goose-girls,' he added untruthfully. 'It would not be fitting or suitable. I am a prince in disguise!'

'You are?' cried the Tramp admiringly. 'Then you're occupying your time, I suppose, in getting up muscle to fight the Dragon.'

The Swineherd's damask cheek grew pale. 'What dragon?' he asked in a stifled voice.

'Oh, any that you chance to meet. All princes, as you yourself must know, have to fight at least one dragon. That is what princes are for.'

'Two-headed?' inquired the Swineherd, gulping.

'Two?' cried the Tramp. 'Seven, you mean! Two-headed dragons are quite out of date.'

The Swineherd felt his heart thump. Suppose, in spite of all the stories, instead of the prince killing the monster, the monster should kill the prince? He was not, you understand, afraid. But he wondered whether, after all, he were not a simple swineherd.

'A fine lot of porkers you've got there!' The Tramp glanced appreciatively from the swine to his piece of sausage.

A snort of disgust went up from the herd. A raggedy tramp to be calling them porkers!

'Perhaps you are not aware,' they grunted, 'that we are sheep in disguise!'

'Oh, dear!' said the Tramp, with a doleful air. 'I'm sorry for you, my friends!'

'Why should you be sorry?' demanded the swine, sticking their snouts in the air.

'Why? Surely you know that the people here are extremely partial to mutton! If they knew there was a flock of sheep – however disguised – in this meadow –' He broke off, shaking his head and sighing. Then he searched among his tattered rags, discovered a piece of plum cake and munched it sombrely.

The swine, aghast, looked at each other. Mutton – what a frightful word! They had thought of themselves as graceful lambs prancing for ever in fields of flowers – never as legs of mutton. Would it not be wiser, they cogitated, to decide to be merely pigs?

'Here, goosey-ganders!' chirruped the Tramp. He tossed his crumbs to the Goose-girl's flock.

The geese, as one bird, raised their heads and let out a snake-like hiss.

'We're swans!' they cackled in high-pitched chorus. And then, as he did not seem to believe them, they added the word, 'Disguised!'

'Well, if that's the case,' the Tramp remarked, 'you won't be here very long. All swans, as you know, belong to the King. Dear me, what lucky birds you are! You will swim on the ornamental lake, and courtiers with golden scissors will clip your flying-feathers. Strawberry jam on silver plates will be given you every morning. And not a care in the world will you have – not even the trouble of hatching your eggs, for these His Majesty eats for breakfast.'

'What!' cried the geese. 'No grubs? No goslings?'

'Certainly not! But think of the honour!' The Tramp chuckled and turned away, bumping into a shaggy shape that was standing among the daisies.

The geese stood rigid in the grass, staring at each other.

Strawberry jam! Clipped wings! No hatching season! Could they have made a mistake, they wondered? Were they not, after all, just geese?

From something that once had been a pocket the Tramp extracted an apple.

'Pardon, friend!' he said to the Ass, as he took a juicy

bite. 'I'd offer you half – but you don't need it. You've all this buttercup field.'

The Ass surveyed the scene with distaste. 'It may be all very well for donkeys, but don't imagine,' he remarked, 'that I'm such an ass as I look. As you may be interested to know, I'm an Arab steed in disguise!'

'Indeed?' The Tramp looked very impressed. 'How you must long, if that is so, for the country of your birth. Sandstorms! Mirages! Waterless deserts!'

'Waterless?' The Ass looked anxious.

'Well, practically. But that's nothing to you. The way you Arab animals can live for weeks on nothing – nothing to eat, nothing to drink, nowhere to sleep – it's wonderful!'

'But what about all those oases? Surely grass grows there?'

'Few and far between,' said the Tramp. 'But what of that, my friend? The less you eat the faster you go! The less you drink the lighter you are! It only takes you half a jiffy to fling yourself down and shelter your master when his enemies attack!'

'But,' cried the Ass, 'in that case, *I* should be shot at first!'

'Naturally,' the Tramp replied. 'That's why one admires you so – you noble Arab steeds. You're ready to die at any moment!'

The Ass rubbed his forehead against his leg. Was he ready to die at any moment? He could not honestly answer Yes. Weeks and weeks with nothing to eat! And here the buttercups and daisies were enough for a dozen asses. He might indeed be an Arab steed – but then again, he mightn't. Up and down went his shaggy head as he pondered the difficult problem.

'That's for you, old Natterjack!' The Tramp tossed the core of his apple under the stepping-stone.

'Don't call me Natterjack!' snapped the Toad.

'Puddocky, then, if you prefer it!'

'Those are the names one gives to toads. *I* am a frog in disguise.'

'Oh, happy creature!' the Tramp exclaimed. 'Sitting on lily-leaves all night, singing a song to the moon.'

'All night? I'd take my death of cold!'

'Catching spiders and dragon-flies for the lady-frog of your choice!'

'None for myself?' the Toad inquired.

'A frog that would a-wooing go – and you are certainly such a one! – wouldn't want to catch for himself!'

The Toad was, however, not so sure. He liked a juicy spider. He was just deciding, after all, that he might as well be a toad, when – plop! – went a pebble right beside him and he hurriedly popped in his head.

'Who threw that?' said the Tramp quickly.

'I did,' came the answer from the bridge. 'Not to hit him! Just to make him jump!'

'Good boy!' The Tramp looked up with a smile. 'A fine, friendly lad like you wouldn't hurt a toad!'

'Of course I wouldn't. Or anything else. But don't you call me boy or lad. I'm really a –'

'Wait! Don't tell me! Let me guess! An Indian? No – a pirate!'

'That's right!' said the Boy, with a curt nod, showing all the gaps in his teeth in a terrible pirate smile. 'If you want to know my name,' he snarled, 'just call me One-eyed Corambo!'

'Got your cutlass?' the Tramp inquired. 'Your skull and crossbones? Your black silk mask? Well, I shouldn't hang about here any longer! Landlubbers aren't worth robbing! Set your course away from the North. Make for Tierra del Fuego.'

'Been there,' the Boy said loftily.

'Well, any other place you like – no pirate lingers long on land. Have you been –' the Tramp lowered his voice, 'have you been to *Dead Man's Drop*?'

The Boy smiled and shook his head.

'That's the place for me,' he cried, reaching for his monkey. 'I'll just go and say good-bye to my mother and –'

'Your mother! Did I hear aright? One-eyed Corambo hopping off to say good-bye to his mother! A pirate captain wasting time by running home – well, really!' The Tramp was overcome with amusement.

The Boy looked at him doubtfully. Where, he wondered, *was* Dead Man's Drop? How long would it take him to go and come? His mother would be anxious. And apart from that – as he'd reason to know – she was making pancakes for supper. It might be better, just for today, to be his outer self. Corambo could wait until to-morrow, Corambo was always there.

'Taking your monkey along as a mascot?' The Tramp looked quizzically at the toy.

He was answered by an angry squeal. 'Don't you call me a monkey!' it jabbered. 'I'm a little boy in disguise!'

'A boy!' cried the Tramp. 'And not at school?'

'School?' said the Monkey nervously. '"Two and two make five," you mean, and all that sort of thing?'

'Exactly,' said the Tramp gravely. 'You'd better hurry along now before they find you're missing. Here!' He scrabbled among his rags, drew two chocolates from under his collar, and offered one to the Monkey.

But the little creature turned its back. School – he hadn't bargained for that. Better, any day of the week, to be a moth-eaten monkey. He felt a sudden rush of love for his old fur coat and his glass eyes and his wrinkled jungle tail.

'You take it, Corambo!' The Tramp grinned. 'Pirates are always hungry.' He handed one chocolate to the Boy and ate the other himself.

'Well,' he said, licking his lips, 'time flies and so must I!' He glanced round at the little group and gave a cheerful nod.

'So long!' He smiled at them rosily. And thrusting his hands among his rags, he brought out a piece of bread and butter, and sauntered away across the bridge.

The Boy gazed after him thoughtfully, with a line across his brow. Then suddenly he threw up his hand.

'Hey!' he cried.

The Tramp paused.

'What is your name? You never told us! Who are *you*?' said the Boy.

'Yes, indeed!' came a score of voices. 'Who are *you*?' the Goose-girl asked; and the Swineherd, the geese, the swine and the Ass echoed the eager question. Even the Toad put out his head and demanded: 'Who are *you*?'

'Me?' cried the Tramp, with an innocent smile. 'If you really want to know,' he said, 'I'm an angel in disguise.'

He bowed to them amid his tatters and waved as he turned away.

'Ha, ha, ha! A jolly good joke!'

The Boy burst into a peal of laughter. Jug-jug-jug! in his throat it went. That tattered old thing an angel!

But suddenly the laugh ceased. The Boy stared, screwed up his eyes, looked again and stared.

The Tramp was skipping along the road, hopping for joy, it seemed. Each time he skipped his feet went higher, and the earth – could it really be true? the Boy wondered – was falling away beneath him. Now he was skimming the tops of the daisies and presently he was over the hedge, skipping higher and higher. Up, up he went and cleared

Up, up he went, plumbing the depths of the sky

the woodland, plumbing the depths of the sky. Then he spread himself on the sunny air and stretched his arms and legs.

And as he did so the tattered rags fluttered along his back. Something, the watchers clearly saw, was pushing them aside.

Then, feather by feather, from under each shoulder, a broad grey pinion showed. Out and out the big plumes stretched, on either side of the Tramp, until he was only a tattered scrap between his lifting wings. They flapped for a moment above the trees, balancing strongly against the air, then with a sweeping sea-gull movement they bore him up and away.

'Oh, dear! Oh, dear!' the Goose-girl sighed, knitting her brows in a frown. For the Tramp had put her in an awkward predicament. She was almost – if not quite – convinced she was not the daughter of a King, and now – well look at him! All those feathers under his rags! If he was an angel, what was she? A goose-girl – or something grander?

Her mind was whirling. Which was true? Shaking her head in bewilderment, she glanced across the stream at the Swineherd, and the sight of him made her burst out laughing. Really, she couldn't help it.

There he sat, gazing up at the sky, with his curls standing on end with surprise, and his eyes as round as soup-plates.

'Ahem!' She gave a delicate cough. 'Perhaps it will not be necessary to fight the Dragon now!'

He turned to her with a startled look. Then he saw that she was smiling gently and his face suddenly cleared. He laughed and leapt across the stream.

'You shall have your golden crown,' he cried. 'I'll make it for you myself!'

'Gold is too heavy,' she said demurely, behind her ferny fan.

'Not my kind of gold.' The Swineherd smiled. He gathered a handful of buttercups, wove them into a little wreath and set it on her head.

And from that moment the question which was once so grave – were they goose-girl and swineherd, or prince and princess? – seemed to them not to matter. They sat there gazing at each other, forgetting everything else.

The geese, who were also quite amazed, glanced from the fading speck in the sky to their neighbours in the meadow.

'Poor pigs!' they murmured mockingly. 'Roast mutton with onion sauce!'

'You'll look pretty foolish,' the swine retorted, 'on an ornamental lake!'

But though they spoke harshly to each other, they could not help feeling, privately, that the Tramp had put them in a very tight corner.

Then an old goose gave a high-pitched giggle.

'What does it matter?' he cackled gaily. 'Whatever we are within ourselves, at least we *look* like geese!'

'True!' agreed an elderly pig. 'And *we* have the shape of swine!'

And at that, as though released from a burden, they all began to laugh. The field rang with their mingled cries and the larks looked down in wonder.

'What does it matter – cackle, cackle! What does it matter – ker-onk, ker-onk!'

'Hee-haw!' said the Ass, as he flung up his head and joined in the merry noise.

'Thinking about your fine oasis?' the Toad inquired sarcastically.

'Hee-haw! Hee-haw! I am indeed! What an ass I was, not to see it before. I've only just realized, Natterjack, that my oasis is not in the desert. Hee-haw! Hee-haw! It's under my hoof – here in this very field.'

'Then you're not an Arab steed after all?' the Toad inquired, with a jeer.

'Ah,' said the Ass, 'I wouldn't say that. But now' – he glanced at the flying figure – 'I'm content with my disguise!'

He snatched at a buttercup hungrily as though he had galloped a long distance through a leafless, sandy land.

The Toad looked up with a wondering eye.

'Could *I* be content with *my* disguise?' He pondered the question gravely. And as he did so a hazel nut fell from a branch above him. It hit his head and bounced off lightly, bobbing away on the stream.

'That would have stunned a frog,' thought the Toad, 'but I, in my horny coat, felt nothing.' A gratified smile, very large and toothy, split his face in the middle. He thrust out his head and craned it upwards.

'Come on with your pebbles, boy!' he croaked. 'I've got my armour on!'

But the Boy did not hear the puddocky challenge. He was leaning back against the bridge, watching the Tramp on his broad wings flying into the sunset. Not with surprise – perhaps he was not yet old enough to be surprised at things – but his eyes had a look of lively interest.

He watched and watched till the sky grew dusky and the first stars twinkled out. And when the little flying speck was no longer even a speck, he drew a long, contented sigh and turned again to the earth.

That he was Corambo, he did not doubt. He had never doubted it. But now he knew he was other things, as well as a one-eyed pirate. And far above all – he rejoiced at it – he was just a barefoot boy. And, moreover, a boy who was feeling peckish and ready for his supper.

'Come on!' he called to the Toy Monkey. He tucked it comfortably under his arm, with its tail around his wrist.

And the two of them kept each other warm as they wandered home together.

The long day fell away behind him to join his other days. All he could think of now was the night. He could sense already the warmth of the kitchen, the sizzling pancakes on the stove and his mother bending above them. Her face, framed in its ring of curls, would be ruddy and weary – like the sun. For, indeed, as he had many times told her, the sun has a mother's face.

And presently, there he was on the doorstep and there was she as he had pictured her. He leaned against her checked apron and broke off a piece of pancake.

'Well, what have you been doing?' she smiled.

'Nothing,' he murmured contentedly.

For he knew – and perhaps she knew it too – that nothing is a useful word. It can mean exactly what you like – anything – everything . . .

The end of the story died away.

Mary Poppins sat still and silent.

Around her lay the motionless children, making never a sound. Her gaze, coming back from the far horizon, flickered across their quiet faces and over the head of the Park Keeper, as it nodded dreamily.

'Humph!' she remarked, with a haughty sniff. 'I recount a chapter of history and you all fall fast asleep!'

'I'm not asleep,' Jane reassured her. 'I'm thinking about the story.'

'I heard every word,' said Michael, yawning.

The Park Keeper rocked, as if in a trance. 'A Nexplorer in disguise,' he murmured, 'sittin' in the midnight sun and climbin' the North Pole!'

'Ouch!' cried Michael, starting up. 'I felt a drop on my nose!'

'And I felt one on my chin,' said Jane.

They rubbed their eyes and looked about them. The syrupy sun had disappeared and a cloud was creeping over the Park. Plop! Plop! Patter, patter! The big drops drummed on the leaves.

The Park Keeper opened his eyes and stared.

'It's rainin'!' he cried in astonishment. 'And me with no umbrella!'

He glanced at the dangling-shape on the bough and darted towards the parrot.

'Oh, no, you don't!' said Mary Poppins. Quick as a needle, she grasped the handle.

'I've a long way to go and me chest is bad and I oughtn't to wet me feet!' The Park Keeper gave her a pleading glance.

'Then you'd better not go to the North Pole!' She snapped the parrot umbrella open and gathered up Annabel. 'The Equator – that's the place for you!' She turned away with a snort of contempt.

'Wake up, John and Barbara, please! Jane and Michael, take the rug and wrap it round yourselves and the Twins.'

Raindrops bigger than sugar-plums were tumbling all about them. They drummed and thumped on the children's heads as they wrapped themselves in the rug.

'We're a parcel!' cried Michael excitedly. 'Tie us up with string, Mary Poppins, and send us through the post!'

'Run!' she commanded, taking no notice. And away they hurried, stumbling and tumbling, over the rainy grass.

The dogs came barking along beside them and, forgetting their promise to Mary Poppins, shook themselves over her skirt.

'All that sun and all this rain! One after another! Who'd 'ave thought it?'

The Park Keeper shook his head in bewilderment. He could still hardly believe it.

'An explorer would!' snapped Mary Poppins. She gave her head a satisfied toss. 'And so would I – so there!'

'Too big for your boots – that's what you are!' The Park Keeper's words were worse than they sounded. For he whispered them into his coat-collar in case she should overhear. But, even so, perhaps she guessed them, for she flung at him a smile of conceit and triumph as she hurried after the children.

Off she tripped through the streaming Park, picking her way among the puddles. Neat and trim as a fashion-plate she crossed Cherry Tree Lane and flitted up the garden path of Number Seventeen . . .

★

Jane emerged from the plaid bundle and patted her soaking hair.

'Oh, bother!' she said. 'I've lost my feather.'

'That settles it, then,' said Michael calmly. 'You can't be Minnehaha!'

He unwound himself and felt in his pocket. 'Ah, here's my ant! I've got him safely!'

'Oh, I don't mean Minnehaha, really – but somebody,' persisted Jane, 'somebody else inside me. I know. I always have the feeling.'

The black ant hurried across the table.

'I don't,' Michael said, as he gazed at it. 'I don't feel anything inside me but my dinner and Michael Banks.'

But Jane was thinking her own thoughts.

'And Mary Poppins,' she went on. 'She's somebody in disguise, too. Everybody is.'

'Oh, no, she's not!' said Michael stoutly. 'I'm absolutely certain!'

A light step sounded on the landing.

'Who's not what?' inquired a voice.

'You, Mary Poppins!' Michael cried. 'Jane says you're somebody in disguise. And *I* say you aren't. You're nobody!'

Her head went up with a quick jerk and her eyes had a hint of danger.

'I hope,' she said, with awful calmness, 'that I did not hear what I *think* I heard. Did you say I was nobody, Michael?'

'Yes! I mean – no!' He tried again. 'I really meant to say, Mary Poppins, that you're not really *any-body*!'

'Oh, indeed?' Her eyes were now as black as a boot-button. 'If I'm not anybody, Michael, who *am* I – I'd like to know!'

'Oh, dear!' he wailed. 'I'm all muddled. You're not *somebody*, Mary Poppins – that's what I'm trying to say.'

Not somebody in her tulip hat! Not somebody in her fine blue skirt! Her reflection gazed at her from the mirror, assuring her that she and it were an elegant pair of somebodies.

'Well!' She drew a deep breath and seemed to grow taller as she spoke. 'You have often insulted me, Michael Banks. But I never thought I would see the day when you'd tell me I wasn't somebody. What am I, then, a painted portrait?'

She took a step towards him.

'I m-m-mean –' he stammered, clutching at Jane. Her hand was warm and reassuring and the words he was looking for leapt to his lips.

'I don't mean somebody, Mary Poppins! I mean not somebody *else*! You're Mary Poppins through and through! Inside and outside. And round about. All of you is Mary Poppins. That is how I like you!'

'Humph!' she said disbelievingly. But the fierceness faded away from her face.

With a laugh of relief he sprang towards her, embracing her wet blue skirt.

'Don't grab me like that, Michael Banks. I'm not a Dutch Doll, thank you!'

'You are!' he shouted. 'No, you're not! You only look like one. Oh, Mary Poppins, tell me truly! You aren't anybody in disguise? I want you just as you are!'

A faint, pleased smile puckered her mouth. Her head gave a prideful toss.

'Me! Disguised! Certainly not!'

With a loud sniff at the mere idea, she disengaged his hands.

'But, Mary Poppins –' Jane persisted. 'Supposing you weren't Mary Poppins, who would you choose to be?'

The blue eyes under the tulip hat turned to her in surprise.

There was only one answer to such a question.

'Mary Poppins!' she said.

CHAPTER TWO

The Faithful Friends

'Faster, please!' said Mary Poppins, tapping on the glass panel with the beak of her parrot-headed umbrella.

Jane and Michael had spent the morning at the Barber's shop, and the Dentist's, and because it was late, as a great treat, they were taking a taxi home.

The Taxi Man stared straight before him and gave his head a shake.

'If I go any faster,' he shouted, 'it'll make me late for me dinner.'

'Why?' demanded Jane, through the window. It seemed such a silly thing to say. Surely, the quicker a Taxi Man drove the earlier he would arrive!

'Why?' echoed the Taxi Man, keeping his eye on the wheel. 'A Naccident – that's why! If I go any faster, I'll run into something – and that'll be a Naccident. And a Naccident – it's plain enough! – will make me late for me dinner. Oh, dear!' he exclaimed, as he put on the brake. 'Red again, I see!'

He turned and put his head through the window. His bulgy eyes and drooping whiskers made him look like a seal.

'There's always trouble at these 'ere signals!' He waved his hand at the stream of cars all waiting for the lights to change.

And now it was Michael who asked him why.

'Don't you know *nothing*?' the Taxi Man cried. 'It's because of the chap on duty!'

He pointed to the signal-box, where a helmeted figure, with his head on his hand, was gazing into the distance.

'Absent-minded – that's what 'e is. Always staring and moping. And 'alf the time 'e forgets the lights. I've known them to stay red for a whole morning. If it's goin' to be like that today, I'll never get me dinner. You 'aven't got a sangwidge on you?' He looked at Michael, hopefully. 'No? Nor yet a chocolate drop?' Jane smiled and shook her head.

The Taxi Man sighed despondently.

'Nobody thinks of nobody these days.'

'*I'm* thinking of someone!' said Mary Poppins. And she looked so stern and disapproving that he turned away in dismay.

'They're green!' he cried, as he looked at the lights. And, huddling nervously over the wheel, he drove along Park Avenue as though pursued by wolves.

Bump! Bump! Rattle! Rattle! The three of them jolted and bounced on their seats.

'Sit up straight!' said Mary Poppins, sliding into a corner. 'You are not a couple of Jack-in-the-boxes!'

'I know I'm not,' said Michael, gasping. 'But I feel like one and my bones are shaking –' He gulped quickly and bit his tongue and left the sentence unfinished. For the taxi had stopped with a frightful jerk and flung them all to the floor.

'Mary Poppins,' said Jane in a muffled voice, 'I think you're *sitting* on me!'

'My foot! My foot! It's caught in something!'

'I'll thank you, Michael,' said Mary Poppins, 'to take it out of my hat!'

She rose majestically from the floor, and seizing her parrot-headed umbrella sprang out on to the pavement.

'Well, you said to go faster,' the Taxi Man muttered, as

she thrust the fare into his hand. She glared at him in offended silence. And in order to escape that look he shrank himself down inside his collar so that nothing was left but his whiskers.

'Don't bother about a tip,' he begged. 'It's really been a p-p-pleasure.'

'I had no intention of bothering!' She opened the gate of Number Seventeen with an angry flick of her hand.

The Taxi Man started up his engine and jerked away down the Lane. 'She's upset me, that's what she's done!' he murmured. 'If I do get home in time for me dinner, I shan't be able to eat it!'

Mary Poppins tripped up the path, followed by Jane and Michael.

Mrs Banks stood in the front hall, looking up at the stairs.

'Oh, do be careful, Robertson Ay!' she was saying anxiously. He was carrying a cardboard box and lurching slowly from stair to stair as though he were almost asleep.

'Never a moment's peace!' he muttered. 'First it's one thing, then another. There!' He gave a sleepy heave, thrust the package into the nursery and fell in a snoring heap on the landing.

Jane dashed upstairs to look at the label.

'What's in it – a present?' shouted Michael.

The Twins, bursting with curiosity, were jumping up and down. And Annabel peered through her cot railings and banged her rattle loudly.

'Is this a nursery or a bear-pit?' Mary Poppins stepped over Robertson Ay as she hurried into the room.

'A bear-pit!' Michael longed to answer. But he caught her eye and refrained.

'Really!' Mrs Banks protested, as she stumbled over Robertson Ay. 'He chooses such inconvenient places! Oh, gently, children! Do be careful! That box belongs to Miss Andrew!'

Miss Andrew! Their faces fell.

'Then it isn't presents!' said Michael blankly. He gave the box a push.

'It's probably full of medicine bottles!' said Jane in a bitter voice.

'It's not,' insisted Mrs Banks. 'Miss Andrew has sent us all her treasures. And I thought, Mary Poppins' – she glanced at the stiff white shape beside her – 'I thought, perhaps, you could keep them here!' She nodded towards the mantelpiece.

Mary Poppins regarded her in silence. If a pin had fallen you could have heard it.

'Am I an octopus?' she inquired, finding her voice at last.

'An octopus?' cried Mrs Banks. Had she ever suggested such a thing? 'Of course you're not, Mary Poppins.'

'Exactly!' Mary Poppins retorted. 'I have only one pair of hands.'

Mrs Banks nodded uneasily. She had never expected her to have more.

'And that one pair has enough to do without dusting *anyone's* treasures.'

'But, Mary Poppins, I never dreamed –' Mrs Banks was

getting more and more flustered. 'Ellen is here to do the dusting. And it's only until Miss Andrew comes back – if, of course, she ever does. She behaved so strangely when she was here. Why are you giggling, Jane?'

But Jane only snickered and shook her head. She remembered the strange behaviour!

'Where has she gone to?' Michael asked.

'She seems to have had some sort of a shock – what are you laughing at, children? – and the doctor has ordered a long voyage, away to the South Seas. She says –' Mrs Banks fished into her pocket and brought out a crumpled letter.

'And while I am away,' she read out, 'I shall leave my valuables with you. Be sure they are put in a safe place where nothing can happen to them. I shall expect, on my return, to find everything exactly as it is – nothing broken, nothing mended. Tell George to wear his overcoat. This weather is changeable.

'So you see, Mary Poppins,' said Mrs Banks, looking up with a flattering smile, 'the nursery does seem the best place. Anything left in *your* charge is always perfectly safe!'

'There's safety *and* safety!' sniffed Mary Poppins. 'And I hope I see further than my nose!' It was tilted upwards, as she spoke, even more than usual.

'Oh, I am sure you do!' murmured Mrs Banks, wondering, for the hundredth time, why Mary Poppins – no matter what the situation – was always so pleased with herself.

'Well, now I think I must go and –' But without saying what she was going to do, she ran out of the nursery, jumped over Robertson Ay's legs and bustled away down the stairs.

'Allow me, Michael, if you please!' Mary Poppins seized his wrist, as he pulled the lid off the box. 'Remember what curiosity did – it killed the cat, you know!'

Her quick hands darted among the papers, and briskly

unwrapped a little bundle. Out came a bird with a chipped nose and a Chelsea china lamb.

'Funny sort of treasures,' said Michael. 'I could mend this bird with a piece of putty But I mustn't – so Miss Andrew said. They're to stay exactly as they are.'

'Nothing does that,' said Mary Poppins, with a priggish look on her face.

'You do!' he insisted gallantly.

She sniffed, and glanced at the nursery mirror. Her reflection gave a similar sort of sniff and glanced at Mary Poppins. Each of them, it was easy to see, highly approved of the other.

'I wonder why she kept this?' Jane took an old cracked tile from the box. The picture showed a boat-load of people rowing towards an island.

'To remind her of her youth,' said Michael.

'To give more trouble,' snapped Mary Poppins, shaking the dust from another wrapping.

Back and forth the children ran, collecting and setting up the treasures – a cottage in a snowstorm, with *Home Sweet Home* on the glass globe; a pottery hen on a yellow nest; a red-and-white china clown; a winged horse of celluloid, prancing on its hind legs; a flower vase in the shape of a swan; a little red fox of carved wood; an egg-shaped piece of polished granite; a painted apple with a boy and a girl playing together inside it; and a roughly made, full-rigged ship in a jam-jar.

'I hope that's all,' grumbled Michael. 'The mantelpiece is crowded.'

'Only one more,' said Mary Poppins, as she drew out a knobbly bundle. A couple of china ornaments came forth from the paper wrapper. Her eyebrows went up as she looked at them and she gave a little shrug. Then she handed one each to Jane and Michael.

Weary of running back and forth, they set the ornaments

hurriedly at either end of the mantelpiece. Then Jane looked at hers and blinked her eyes.

A china lion, with his paw on the chest of a china huntsman, was reclining beneath a banana tree which, of course, was also china. The man and the animal leaned together, smiling blissfully. Never, thought Jane, in all her life, had she seen two happier creatures.

'He reminds me of somebody!' she exclaimed, as she gazed at the smiling huntsman. Such a manly figure he looked, too, in his spruce blue jacket and black top-boots.

'Yes,' agreed Michael. 'Who can it be?'

44

He frowned as he tried to recall the name. Then he looked at his half of the china pair and gave a cry of dismay.

'Oh, Jane! *What* a pity! My lion has lost his huntsman!'

It was true. There stood another banana tree, there sat another painted lion. But in the other huntsman's place there was only a gap of roughened china. All that remained of his manly shape was one black shiny boot.

'Poor lion!' said Michael. 'He looks so sad!'

And, indeed, there was no denying it. Jane's lion was wreathed in smiles, but his brother had such a dejected look that he seemed to be almost in tears.

'*You'll* be looking sad in a minute – unless you get ready for lunch!'

Mary Poppins' face was so like her voice that they ran to obey her without a word.

But they caught a glimpse, as they rushed away, of her starched white figure standing there, with its arms full of crumpled paper. She was gazing with a reflective smile at Miss Andrew's broken treasure – and it seemed to them that her lips moved.

Michael gave Jane a fleeting grin.

'I expect she's only saying "Humph!" '

But Jane was not so sure . . .

'Let's go to the swings,' suggested Michael, as they hurried across the Lane after lunch.

'Oh, no! The Lake. I'm tired of swinging.'

'Neither swings nor lakes,' said Mary Poppins. 'We are taking the Long Walk!'

'Oh, Mary Poppins,' grumbled Jane, 'the Long Walk's far too long!'

'I can't walk all that way,' said Michael. 'I've eaten much too much.'

The Long Walk stretched across the Park from the Lane to the Far Gate, linking the little countrified road to the busy streets they had travelled that morning. It was wide and straight and uncompromising – not like the narrow, curly paths that led to the Lake, and the Playground. Trees and fountains bordered it, but it always seemed to Jane and Michael at least ten miles in length.

'The Long Walk – or the short walk home! Take your choice!' Mary Poppins warned them.

Michael was just about to say he would go home, when Jane ran on ahead.

'I'll race you,' she cried, 'to the first tree!'

Michael could never bear to be beaten. 'That's not

fair! You had a good start!' And off he dashed at her heels.

'Don't expect *me* to keep up with you! I am not a centipede!'

Mary Poppins sauntered along, enjoying the balmy air, and assuring herself that the balmy air was enjoying Mary Poppins. How could it do otherwise, she thought, when under her arm was the parrot umbrella and over her wrist a new black hand-bag?

The perambulator creaked and groaned. In it, the Twins and Annabel, packed as close as birds in a nest, were playing with the blue duck.

'That's cheating, Michael!' grumbled Jane. For accidentally on purpose, he had pushed her aside and was running past.

From tree to tree they raced along, first one ahead and then the other, each of them trying to win. The Long Walk streamed away behind them and Mary Poppins and the perambulator were only specks in the distance.

'Next time you push me I'll give you a punch!' said Michael, red in the face.

'If you bump into me again I'll pull your hair, Michael!'

'Now, now!' the Park Keeper warned them sternly. 'Observe the rules! No argle-bargling!'

He was meant to be sweeping up the twigs, but, instead, he was chatting with the Policeman, who was leaning against a maple-tree, whiling away his time.

Jane and Michael stopped in their tracks. Their race, they were both surprised to find, had brought them right across the Park and near to the Far Gate.

The Park Keeper looked at them severely. 'Always argufying!' he said. 'I never did that when *I* was a boy. But then I was a Nonly child, just me and me poor old mother. I never 'ad nobody to play with. You two don't know when you're lucky!'

'Well, I dunno!' the Policeman said. 'Depends on how you look at it. I had someone to play with, you might say, but it never did *me* any good!'

'Brothers or sisters?' Jane inquired, all her crossness vanishing. She liked the Policeman very much. And today he seemed to remind her of someone, but she couldn't think who it was.

'Brothers!' the Policeman informed her, without enthusiasm.

'Older or younger?' Michael asked. Where, he wondered to himself, had he seen another face like that?

'Same age,' replied the Policeman flatly.

'Then you must have been twins, like John and Barbara!'

'I was triplets,' the Policeman said.

'How lovely!' cried Jane, with a sigh of envy.

'Well, it wasn't so lovely, not to *my* mind. The opposite, I'd say. "Egbert," my mother was always asking, "why don't you play with Herbert and Albert?" But it wasn't me – it was *them* that wouldn't. All they wanted was to go to the Zoo, and when they came back they'd be animals – tigers tearing about the house and letting on it was Timbuctoo or around the Gobi Desert. *I* never wanted to be a tiger. I liked playing bus-conductors and keeping things neat and tidy.'

'Like 'er!' The Park Keeper waved to a distant fountain where Mary Poppins was leaning over to admire the set of her hat.

'Like her,' agreed the Policeman, nodding. 'Or,' he said, grinning, 'that nice Miss Ellen.'

'Ellen's not neat,' protested Michael. 'Her hair straggles and her feet are too big.'

'And when they grew up,' demanded Jane, 'what did Herbert and Albert do?' She liked to hear the end of a story

'Do?' said the Policeman, very surprised. 'What one

triplet does, the others do. They joined the police, of course!'

'But I thought you were all so different!'

'We were and we are!' the Policeman argued. 'Seeing as how I stayed in London and they went off to distant lands. Wanted to be near the jungle, they said, and mix with giraffes and leopards. One of 'em – Herbert – he never came back. Just sent a note saying not to worry. "I'm happy," he said, "and I feel at home!" And after that, never a word – not even a card at Christmas.'

'And what about Albert?' the children prompted.

'Ah – Albert – yes! He did come back. After he met with his accident.'

'What accident?' they wanted to know. They were burning with curiosity.

'Lorst his foot,' the Policeman answered. 'Wouldn't say how, or why or where. Just got himself a wooden one and never smiled again. Now he works on the traffic signals. Sits in his box and pines away. And sometimes –' The Policeman lowered his voice. 'Sometimes he *forgets* the lights. Leaves them at red for a whole day till London's at a standstill!'

Michael gave an excited skip. 'He must be the one we passed this morning, in the box by the Far Gate!'

'That's him all right!' The Policeman nodded.

'But what is he pining for?' asked Jane. She wanted every detail.

'For the jungle, he keeps on telling me. He says he's got a friend there!'

'A funny place to 'ave a friend!' The Park Keeper glanced around the Park to see that all was in order.

'T'chah!' he exclaimed disgustedly. 'That's Willerby up to 'is tricks again! Look at 'im sittin' up there on the wall! Come down out of that! Remember the bye-laws! No dogs allowed on the Park Wall. I shall 'ave to speak to

Miss Lark,' he muttered, 'feedin' 'im all that dainty food! 'E's twice the size he was yesterday!'

'That's not Willoughby!' said Michael. 'It's a much, much larger dog.'

'It isn't a dog at all!' cried Jane. 'It's a –'

'Lumme! You're right!' The Policeman stared. 'It's not a dog – it's a lion!'

'Oh, what shall I do?' wailed the Park Keeper. 'Nothing like this ever 'appened before, not even when I was a boy!'

'Go and get someone from the Zoo – it must have escaped from there! Here, you two –' the Policeman cried. He caught the children and swung them up to the top of a near-by fountain. 'You stay there while I head him off!'

'Observe the rules!' shrieked the Park Keeper. 'No lions allowed in the Park!' He gave one look at the tawny shape and ran in the opposite direction.

The Lion swung his head about, glancing along Cherry Tree Lane and then across the lawns. Then he leapt from the wall with a swift movement and made for the Long Walk. His curly mane blew out in the breeze like a large lacy collar.

'Take care!' cried Jane to the Policeman, as he darted forward with arms outspread. It would be sad indeed, she felt, if that manly figure were gobbled up.

'Gurrrr!' the Policeman shouted fiercely.

His voice was so loud and full of warning that everyone in the Park was startled.

Miss Lark, who was knitting by the Lake, came hurrying to the Long Walk with her dogs in close attendance.

'Such a commotion!' she twittered shrilly. 'Whatever is the matter? Oh!' she cried, running round in a circle. 'What shall I do? It's a wild beast! Send for the Prime Minister!'

'Get up a tree!' the Policeman yelled, shaking his fist at the Lion.

'Which tree? Oh, how undignified!'

'That one!' screamed Michael, waving his hand.

Gulping and panting, Miss Lark climbed up, her hair catching in every twig and her knitting wool winding around her legs.

'Andrew and Willoughby, come up, please!' she called down, anxiously. But the dogs were not going to lose their heads. They composed themselves at the foot of the tree and waited to see what would happen.

By this time everyone in the Park had become aware of the Lion. Terrified shouts rang through the air as people swung themselves into the branches or hid behind seats or statues.

'Call out the Firemen!' they all cried. 'Tell the Lord Mayor! Send for a rope!'

But the Lion noticed none of them. He crossed the lawn in enormous leaps, making direct for the blue serge shape of the Officer of the Law.

'Gurrrr, I said!' the Policeman roared, taking out his baton.

The Lion merely tossed his head and flung himself into a crouching position. A ripple ran through all his muscles as he made ready to spring.

'Oh, save him, somebody!' cried Jane, with an anxious glance at the manly figure.

'Help!' screamed a voice from every tree.

'Prime Minister!' cried Miss Lark again.

And then the Lion sprang. He sped like an arrow through the air and landed beside the big black boots.

'Be off, I say!' the Policeman shouted, in a last protesting cry.

But as he spoke a strange thing happened. The Lion rolled over on his back and waved his legs in the air.

'Just like a kitten,' whispered Michael. But he held Jane's hand a little tighter.

'Away with you!' the Policeman bellowed, waving his baton again.

But as though the words were as sweet as music, the Lion put out a long red tongue and licked the Policeman's boots.

'Stop it, I tell you! Get along off!'

But the Lion only wagged its tail and, springing up on its hind legs, it clasped the blue serge jacket.

'Help! Oh, help!' the Policeman gasped.

'Coming!' croaked a hoarse voice, as the Park Keeper crawled to the edge of the Walk with an empty litter-basket over his head.

Beside him crept a small thin man with a butterfly net in his hand.

'I brought the Keeper of the Zoological Gardens!' the Park Keeper hissed at the Policeman. 'Go on!' he urged the little man. 'It's your property – take it away!'

The Keeper of the Zoological Gardens darted behind a fountain. He took a careful look at the Lion as it hugged the dark blue waist.

'Not one of ours!' He shook his head. 'It's far too red and curly. Seems to know *you*!' he called to the Policeman. 'What are you – a lion-tamer?'

'Never saw him before in my life!' The head in the helmet turned aside.

'Oh, wurra! wurra!' the Lion growled, in a voice that held a note of reproach.

'Will nobody send for the Prime Minister?' Miss Lark's voice shrilled from her maple bough.

'I have been sent for, my dear madam!' a voice observed from the next tree. An elderly gentleman in striped trousers was scrambling into the branches.

'Then *do* something!' ordered Miss Lark in a frenzy.

'Shoo!' said the Prime Minister earnestly, waving his hat at the Lion.

But the Lion bared its teeth in a grin as it hugged the Policeman closer.

The Lion . . . clasped the blue serge jacket

'Now, what's the trouble? Who sent for me?' cried a loud, impatient voice.

The Lord Mayor hurried along the Walk with his Aldermen at his heels.

'Good gracious! What are you doing, Smith?' He stared in disgust at the Park Keeper. 'Come out of that basket and stand up straight! It is there to be used for litter, Smith, and not some foolish game.

'I'm usin' it for armour, your Worship! There's a lion in the Park!'

'A lion, Smith? What nonsense you talk! The lions are in the Zoo!'

'A lion?' echoed the Aldermen. 'Ha, ha! What a silly story!'

'It's true!' yelled Jane and Michael at once. 'Look out! He's just behind you!'

The three portly figures turned, and their faces grew pale as marble.

The Lord Mayor waved a feeble hand at the trembling Aldermen.

'Get me water! Wine! Hot milk!' he moaned.

But for once the Aldermen disobeyed. Hot milk indeed! they seemed to say as they dragged him to the Prime Minister's tree and pushed him into the branches.

'Police! Police!' the Lord Mayor cried, catching hold of a bough.

'I'm here, your Honour!' the Policeman panted, pushing away a tawny paw.

But the Lion took this for a mark of affection.

'Gurrrrumph!' he said in a husky voice, as he clasped the Policeman tighter.

'Oh, dear! Oh, dear!' Miss Lark wailed. 'Has nobody got a gun?'

'A dagger! A sword! A crowbar!' cried the voices from every tree.

The Park was ringing with shouts and screams. The Park Keeper rattled his stick on the litter-basket. 'Yoo-hoo!' cried the Keeper of the Zoological Gardens to distract the Lion's attention. The Lion was growling. The Policeman was yelling. The Lord Mayor and the Aldermen were still crying 'Police!'

Then suddenly a silence fell. And a neat, trim figure appeared on the path. Straight on she came, as a ship into port, with the perambulator wheeling before her and the tulip standing up stiff on her hat.

Creak went the wheels.

Tap went her shoes.

And the watching faces grew pale with horror as she tripped towards the Lion.

'Go back, Mary Poppins!' screamed Miss Lark, breaking the awful silence. 'Save yourself and the little ones! There's a wild beast down on the path!'

Mary Poppins looked up at Miss Lark's face as it hung like a fruit among the leaves.

'Go back? When I've only just come out?' She smiled a superior smile.

'Away! Away!' The Prime Minister warned her. 'Take care of those children, woman!'

Mary Poppins gave him a glance so icy that he felt himself freeze to the bough.

'I *am* taking care of these children, thank you. And as for the wild beasts –' She gave a sniff. 'They seem to be all in the trees!'

'It's a lion, Mary Poppins, look!' Michael pointed a trembling finger – and she turned and beheld the two locked figures.

The Policeman now was ducking sideways to prevent the Lion licking his cheek. His helmet was off and his face was pale, but he still had a plucky look in his eye.

'I might have known it!' said Mary Poppins, as she

stared at the curious pair. 'Rover!' she called in exaspera-
tion. 'What do you think you're doing?'

From under his lacy, flopping mane the Lion pricked
up an ear.

'Rover!' she called again. 'Down, I say!'

The Lion gave one look at her and dropped with a thud
to the ground. Then he gave a little throaty growl and
bounded away towards her.

'Oh, the Twins! He'll eat them! Help!' cried Jane.

But the Lion hardly looked at the Twins. He was fawn-
ing at Mary Poppins. He rolled his eyes and wagged his
tail and arched himself against her skirt. Then away he
rushed to the Policeman, seized the blue trousers between
his teeth and tugged them towards the perambulator.

'Don't be so silly!' said Mary Poppins. 'Do as I tell you!
Let him go! You've got the wrong one.'

The Lion loosed the trouser-leg and rolled his eyes in
surprise.

'Do you mean,' the Prime Minister called from his
bough, 'he's to eat *another* Policeman?'

Mary Poppins made no reply. Instead, she fished inside
her handbag and brought out a silver whistle. Then, setting it daintily to her lips, she puffed out her cheeks and
blew.

'Why – *I* could have blown *my* whistle' – the Policeman
stared at the silver shape – 'if only I'd thought of it.'

She turned upon him a look of scorn. 'The trouble with
you is that you don't think. Neither do you!' she snapped
at the Lion.

He hung his head between his paws and looked very
hurt and foolish.

'You don't listen, either,' she added severely. 'In at one
ear and out of the next. There was no need to make such a
foolish mistake.'

The Lion's tail crept between his legs.

'You're careless, thoughtless and inattentive. You ought to be thoroughly ashamed of yourself.'

The Lion gave a humble snuffle as though he agreed with her.

'Who whistled?' called a voice from the Gate. 'Who summoned an Officer of the Law?'

Along the Walk came another policeman, limping unevenly. His face had a melancholy look, as though he possessed a secret sorrow.

'I can't stay long whatever it is,' he said, as he reached the group. 'I left the lights when I heard the whistle and I must get back to them. Why, Egbert!' he said to the First Policeman, 'what's the matter with you?'

'Oh, nothing to complain of, Albert! I've just been attacked by a lion!'

'Lion?' The sad face grew a shade more cheerful as the Second Policeman glanced about him. 'Oh, what a beauty!' he exclaimed, limping towards the tawny shape at Mary Poppins' side.

Jane turned to whisper in Michael's ear.

'He must be the Policeman's brother – the one with the wooden foot!'

'Nice lion! Pretty lion!' said the Second Policeman softly.

And the Lion, at the sound of his voice, leapt to his feet with a roar.

'Now gently, gently! Be a good lion. He's an elegant fellow, so he is!' the Second Policeman crooned.

Then he put back the mane from the Lion's brow and met the golden eyes. A shudder of joy ran through his frame.

'Rover! My dear old friend! It's you!' He flung out his arms with a loving gesture and the Lion rushed into them.

'Oh, Rover! After all these years!' the Second Policeman sobbed.

'Wurra, wurra!' the Lion growled, licking the tears away.

And for a whole minute it was nothing but Rover – Wurra, Rover – Wurra, while they hugged and kissed each other.

'But how did you get here? How did you find me?' demanded the Second Policeman.

'Woof! Burrum!' replied the Lion, nodding towards the perambulator.

'No! You don't say! How very kind! We must always be grateful, Rover! And if I can do you a good turn, Miss Poppins –'

'Oh, get along, do – the pair of you!' said Mary Poppins snappily. For the Lion had rushed to lick her hand and darted back to his friend.

'Woof? Wurra-woof?' he said in a growl.

'Will I come with you? What do you think? As if I could ever leave you again!' And flinging his arm round the Lion's shoulders, the Second Policeman turned.

'Hey!' cried the First Policeman sternly. 'Where are you going to, may I ask? And where are you taking that animal?'

'He's taking *me!*' cried the Second Policeman. 'And we're going where we belong!' His gloomy face had quite changed. It was now rosy and gay.

'But what about the traffic lights? Who's going to look after those?'

'They're all at green!' said the Second Policeman. 'No more signals for me, Egbert! The traffic can do what it likes!'

He looked at the Lion and roared with laughter, and the two of them turned away. Over the lawns they sauntered, chatting – the Lion on its hind legs and the Policeman limping a little. When they came to the Lane Gate they paused for a moment and waved. Then through they went and shut it behind them, and the watchers saw them no more.

The Keeper of the Zoological Gardens gathered up his net.

'I hope they're not making for the Zoo. We haven't a cage to spare!'

'Well, as long as he's out of the public Park –' The Prime Minister clambered out of the tree.

'Haven't we met before?' he inquired, as he took off his hat to Mary Poppins. 'I'm afraid I've forgotten where it was!'

'Up in the air! On a red balloon!' She bowed in a ladylike manner.

'Ah, yes! Hurrrmph!' He seemed rather embarrassed. 'Well – I must be off and make some more laws!'

And, glancing round to make sure the Lion was not coming back, he made for the Far Gate.

'Constable!' cried the Lord Mayor, as he swung himself down from his branch. 'You must go at once to the signal box and switch the lights to red. The traffic can do as it likes, indeed! Whoever heard of such a thing!'

The Policeman, mopping up his scratches, gallantly sprang to attention.

'Very good, your Honour!' he said smartly, and marched away down the Walk.

'As for you, Smith, this is all your fault. Your duty is to look after the Park! But what do I find when I pass this way? Wild animals running all over it. You disappoint me again and again. I must mention it to the King.'

The Park Keeper fell on his knees with a groan.

'Oh, *please* don't mention it, Your Honour! Think of me poor old mother!'

'You should have thought of her yourself before you let that Lion in!'

'But I never let 'im in, Your Worship! It wasn't my fault 'e came over the wall. If anyone's to blame, it's –' The Park Keeper broke off nervously, but he looked in Mary Poppins' direction.

So did the Lord Mayor.

'Aha!' he exclaimed, with a gracious smile. 'Charmed to meet you again, Miss – er –?'

'Poppins,' said Mary Poppins politely.

'Poppins – ah, yes! A charming name! Now, if Smith were only *you*, Miss Poppins, these things would never occur!'

With a bow, the Lord Mayor turned away and billowed down the Walk. The two Aldermen also bowed, and billowed along behind him.

'That's all *you* know!' said the Park Keeper, as he watched them disappear. 'If I was 'er – ha, ha, that's funny! – *anything* could happen!'

'If I were *you*, I'd straighten my tie,' said Mary Poppins

primly. 'Get down from that fountain, Jane and Michael!' She glanced at their grimy knees and faces. 'You look like a couple of Blackamoors!'

'We can't all be like you, you know!' the Park Keeper said sarcastically.

'No,' she agreed. 'And more's the pity!' She pushed the perambulator forward.

'But, Mary Poppins –' Michael burst out. He was longing to ask her about the Lion.

'Butting's for goats – not human beings! Best foot forward, please!'

'It's no use, Michael,' whispered Jane. 'You know she never explains.'

But Michael was too excited to heed.

'Well, if I can't talk about the Lion, will you let me blow your whistle?'

'Certainly not!' She sauntered on.

'I wonder, Mary Poppins,' he cried, 'if you'll ever let me do *anything*!'

'I wonder!' she said, with a mocking smile.

Twilight was falling over the Park. People were scrambling out of the trees and hurrying home to safety.

From the Far Gate came a frightful din. And looking through it the children saw a motionless block of traffic. The lights were red, the horns were hooting and the drivers were shaking their fists.

The Policeman was calmly surveying the scene. He had been given an order and he was obeying it.

'Has your brother Albert gone for good?' cried Jane, as he waved to them.

'No idea,' he replied calmly. 'And it's no affair of mine!'

Then round the perambulator swung and they all went back by the Long Walk. The Twins and Annabel, weary of playing with the blue duck, let it drop over the side. Nobody noticed. Jane and Michael were far too busy thinking about the day's adventure. And Mary Poppins was far too busy thinking about Mary Poppins.

'I wonder where Albert's gone?' murmured Michael as he strolled along beside her.

'How should *I* know?' she answered, shrugging.

'I thought you knew everything!' he retorted. 'I meant it politely, Mary Poppins!'

Her face, which was just about to be fierce, took on a conceited expression.

'Maybe I do,' she said smugly, as she hurried them across the Lane and in through the front gate . . .

'Oh, Ellen!' Mrs Banks was saying, as they all came into the hall. 'Would you dust the mantelpiece while you're there? Well, darlings?' She greeted the children gaily.

Ellen, half-way up the stairs, replied with a loud sneeze. 'A-tishoo!' She had Hay Fever. She was carrying mugs of milk on a tray and they rattled each time she sneezed.

'Oh, go on, Ellen! You're so *slow*!' said Michael impatiently.

'You hard-hearted – a-tishoo!' she cried, as she dumped the tray on the nursery table.

Helter-skelter they all ran in, as Ellen took a cloth from her pocket and began to dust Miss Andrew's treasures

'Rock cakes for supper! I'll have the biggest!' cried Michael greedily.

Mary Poppins was buttoning on her apron. 'Michael Banks –' she began in a warning voice. But the sentence was never finished.

'Oh, help!' A wild scream rent the air and Ellen fell backwards against the table.

Bang! went the milk mugs on to the floor.

'It's *him*!' shrieked Ellen. 'Oh, what shall I do?' She stood in a running stream of milk and pointed to the mantelpiece.

'What's him? Who's him?' cried Jane and Michael. 'Whatever's the matter, Ellen?'

'There! Under that banana bush! His very self! A-tishoo!'

She was pointing straight at Miss Andrew's huntsman as he smiled in the arms of his Lion.

'Why, of course!' cried Jane, as she looked at the huntsman. 'He's exactly like Egbert – our Policeman!'

'The only one I ever loved, and now a wild beast's got him!'

Ellen flung out a frenzied arm and knocked the teapot over. 'A-tishoo!' she sneezed, distractedly, as she hurried sobbing from the room and thundered down the stairs.

'What a silly she is!' said Michael, laughing. 'As if he'd have turned into china! Besides, we saw him a moment ago, away by the Far Gate!'

'Yes, she's a silly,' Jane agreed. 'But he's very like the huntsman, Michael –' She smiled at the smiling china face. 'And both such manly figures . . .'

'Well, Constable?' said Mr Banks, as he came up the garden path that evening. He wondered if he had broken a bye-law when he saw the policeman at the door.

'It's about the duck!' The Policeman smiled.

'We don't keep ducks,' said Mr Banks. 'Good heavens! What have you done to your face?'

The Policeman patted his bruised cheek. 'Just a scratch,' he murmured modestly. 'But now, that there blue duck –'

'Whoever heard of a blue duck? Go and ask Admiral Boom!'

The Policeman gave a patient sigh and handed over a dingy object.

'Oh, that thing!' Mr Banks exclaimed. 'I suppose the children dropped it!' He stuffed the blue duck into his pocket and opened the front door.

It was at this moment that Ellen, her face hidden in her duster, hurled herself down the front stairs and straight into his arms.

'A-tishoo!' She sneezed so violently that Mr Banks' bowler hat fell off.

'Why, Ellen! What on earth's the matter?' Mr Banks staggered beneath her weight.

'He's gone right into that bit of china!' Her shoulders heaved as she sobbed out the news.

'You're going to China?' said Mr Banks. 'Well, don't be so depressed about it? My dear,' he remarked to Mrs Banks, who was hurrying up the kitchen stairs. 'Ellen is feeling upset, she says, because she is going to China!'

'China?' cried Mrs Banks, raising her eyebrows.

'No! It's *him* that's gorn!' insisted Ellen. 'Under a banana in the African jungle!'

'Africa!' Mr Banks exclaimed, catching only a word here and there. 'I made a mistake,' he said to Mrs Banks. 'She's going to Africa!'

Mrs Banks seemed quite stupefied.

'I'm not! I'm not!' shrieked Ellen wildly.

'Well, wherever you're going, do make up your mind!' Mr Banks thrust her towards a chair.

'Allow me, sir!' the Policeman murmured, stepping into the hall.

Ellen looked up at the sound of his voice and gave a strangled sob.

'*Egbert!* But I thought you were up on the mantelpiece – and a wild beast going to eat you!' She flung out her arm towards the nursery.

'Mantelpiece?' Mr Banks exclaimed.

'A wild beast?' murmured Mrs Banks. Could they – they wondered – believe their ears?

'Leave it to me,' the Policeman said. 'I'll take her a turn along the path. Perhaps it will clear her head.'

He heaved Ellen out of the chair and led her, still gaping, through the door.

Mr Banks mopped his beaded brow. 'Neither China,

nor Africa,' he murmured. 'Merely to the front gate with the Policeman. I never knew that his name was Egbert! Well, I'll just go and say good night to the children . . . All well, Mary Poppins?' he asked gaily, as he sauntered into the nursery.

She gave a conceited toss of her head. Could all be anything but well while *she* was about the house?

Mr Banks glanced contentedly at the roomful of rosy children. Then his eye fell on the mantelpiece and he gave a start of surprise.

'Hullo!' he exclaimed. 'Where did those things come from?'

'Miss Andrew!' all the children answered.

'Quick – let me escape!' Mr Banks turned pale. 'Tell her I've run away! Gone to the moon!'

'She's not here, Daddy,' they reassured him. 'She's far away in the South Seas. And these are all her treasures.'

'Well, I hope she stays there – right at the bottom! *Her* treasures, you say! Well this one isn't!' Mr Banks marched to the mantelpiece and picked up the celluloid horse. I won him myself at an Easter Fair when I was a little boy. Ah, there's my friend, the soapstone bird! A thousand years old, she said it was. And, look, *I* made that little ship. Aren't you proud of your father?'

Mr Banks smiled at his cleverness as he glanced along the mantelpiece.

'I feel like a boy again,' he said. 'These things all come from my old schoolroom. That hen used to warm my breakfast egg. And the fox and the clown and *Home Sweet Home* – how well I remember them! And there – bless their hearts! – are the Lion and Huntsman. I always called them the Faithful Friends. Used to be a pair of these fellows, but they weren't complete, I remember. The second huntsman was broken off, nothing left of him but his boot. Ah! *There's* the other – the broken one. Good gracious!' He gave a start of surprise. '*Both* the huntsmen are here!'

They looked at the broken ornament and blinked with astonishment.

For there, where the blank white gap had been, was a second smiling figure. Beneath the banana tree he sat, leaning – like his unbroken brother – against a shaggy shape. A paw lay lovingly on his breast and his lion – only this morning so sad and tearful – was now showing all his teeth in a grin.

The two ornaments were exactly alike – the two trees bore the same fruit, the two lions were equally happy and the two huntsmen smiled. Exactly alike – but for one exception. For the second huntsman had a crack in his leg just above his boot – the sort of crack you always find when two pieces of broken china are carefully fitted together.

A smile swept over Jane's face as she realized what had happened. She gently touched the crack with her fingers.

'It's Albert, Michael! Albert and Rover! And the other' – she touched the unbroken pair – 'the other must be Herbert!'

Michael's head nodded backwards and forwards like the head of a mandarin.

The questions rose in them like bubbles and they turned to Mary Poppins.

But just as the words leapt to their tongues she silenced them with a look.

'Extraordinary thing,' Mr Banks was saying. 'I could have sworn one figure was missing. It just goes to show – I'm getting older. Losing my memory, I'm afraid. Well, what are you two so amused about?'

'Nothing!' they gurgled, as they flung back their heads and burst into peals of laughter. How could they assure him that his memory was as good as ever it was? How explain the afternoon's adventure, or tell him that they knew now where the Second Policeman had gone? Some things there are that are past telling. And it's no use trying – as they knew very well – to say what cannot be said.

'It's a long time,' grumbled Mr Banks, 'since *I* could laugh at nothing!'

But he looked quite cheerful as he kissed them and went downstairs to dinner.

'Let's put them side by side,' said Jane, setting the little cracked huntsman next to his crackless brother. 'Now they're *both* at home!'

Michael looked up at the mantelpiece and gave a contented chuckle.

'But what will Miss Andrew say, I wonder? Everything was to be kept safe – nothing broken, nothing mended. You don't think she'll separate them, Jane?'

'Just let her try!' said a voice behind them. 'Safe she said they were to be, and safe they are going to stay!'

Mary Poppins was standing on the hearthrug with the teapot in her hand. And her manner was so belligerent that for half a second Jane and Michael felt sorry for Miss Andrew.

She looked from them to the mantelpiece, glancing from their living faces to the smiling china figures.

'One and one makes two,' she declared. 'And two halves make a whole. And Faithful Friends should be together, never kept apart. But, of course, if you don't approve, Michael –' for his face had assumed a thoughtful expression. 'If you think they'd be safe somewhere else – If you like to go to the South Seas and ask Miss Andrew's permission –'

'You know I approve, Mary Poppins!' he cried. 'And I don't want to go to the South Seas. I was only thinking –' He hesitated. 'Well – if *you* hadn't been there, Mary Poppins, do you think they'd have found each other?'

She stood there like a pillar of starch. He was almost sorry he had spoken, she looked so stern and priggish.

'Ifs and whys and buts and hows – you want too much,' she said. But her blue eyes gave a sudden sparkle, and a pleased smile – very like those on the huntsmen's faces – trembled about her lips.

At the sight of it Michael forgot his question. Only that sparkle mattered.

'Oh, be my lion, Mary Poppins! Put your paw around me!'

'And me!' cried Jane as she turned to join them.

Her arms came lightly across their shoulders as she drew them close to the starched apron. And there they were, the three of them, embracing under the nursery lamplight as though beneath a banana tree.

With a little push, Michael spun them round. And again a push. And again a spin. And soon they were all revolving gently in the middle of the room.

'Michael,' said Mary Poppins severely, 'I am not a merry-go-round!'

But he only laughed and hugged her tighter.

'The Faithful Friends are together,' he cried. '*All* the Faithful Friends!'

CHAPTER THREE

Lucky Thursday

'It's dod fair!' grumbled Michael.

He pressed his nose to the window-pane and sniffed a tear away. And, as if to taunt him, a gust of rain rattled against the glass.

All day the storm had raged. And Michael, because he had a cold, was not allowed to go out. Jane and the Twins had put on gum-boots and gone to play in the Park. Even Annabel, wrapped in a mackintosh, had sailed off under the parrot umbrella, looking as proud as a queen.

Oh, how lonely Michael felt! It was Ellen's Day Out. His mother had gone shopping. Mrs Brill was down in the kitchen. And Robertson Ay, up in the attic, was asleep in a cabin trunk.

'Get up and play in your dressing-gown. But don't put a toe outside the nursery!' Mary Poppins had warned him.

So there he was, all by himself, with nothing to do but grumble. He built a castle with his blocks, but it tumbled down when he blew his nose. He tried cutting his hair with his penknife, but the blade was far too blunt. And at last there was nothing left to do but breathe on the rainy window-pane and draw a picture there.

The nursery clock ticked the day away. The weather grew wetter and Michael grew crosser.

But then, at sunset, the clouds lifted and a line of crimson shone from the West. Everything glittered in rain and sun. Rat-tat-tat – on the black umbrellas, the cherry-trees dropped their weight of water. The shouts of Jane and John and Barbara floated up to the window. They were playing leap-frog over the gutters on their way home from the Park.

Admiral Boom came splashing past, looking like a shiny sunflower in his big yellow sou'wester.

The Ice Cream Man trundled along the lane, with a waterproof cape spread over his tricycle. And in front of it the notice said:

DON'T STOP ME
I WANT MY TEA

He glanced at Number Seventeen and waved his hand to the window. Michael, on any other day, would gladly have answered back. But today he deliberately took no notice. He huddled on the window-seat, glumly watching the sunset, and looking over Miss Lark's roof at the first faint star in the sky.

'The others ged all the fud,' he sniffed. 'I wish *I* could have sobe luck!'

Then footsteps clattered on the stairs. The door burst open and Jane ran in.

'Oh, Michael, it was lovely!' she cried. 'We were up to our knees in water.'

'Thed I hobe you catch a code!' he snapped. He gave a guilty glance round to see if Mary Poppins had heard. She was busy unwrapping Annabel and shaking the rain from her parrot umbrella.

'Don't be cross. We all missed you,' said Jane in a coaxing voice.

But Michael did not want to be coaxed. He wanted to be as cross as he liked. Nobody, if he could help it, was going to alter his bad mood. Indeed, he was almost enjoying it.

'Dode touch be, Jade. You're all wet!' he said in a sulky voice.

'So are we!' chirped John and Barbara, running across to hug him.

'Oh, go away!' he cried angrily, turning back to the window. 'I dode want to talk to any of you. I wish you'd all leave be alode!'

'Miss Lark's roof is made of gold!' Jane gazed out at the sunset. 'And there's the first star – wish on it! How does the tune go, Michael?'

He shook his head and wouldn't tell, so she sang the song herself.

'Star light
Star bright.
First star I've seen tonight,
Wish I may
Wish I might
That the wish may come true
That I wish tonight.'

She finished the song and looked at the star.

'I've wished,' she whispered, smiling.

'It's easy for *you* to sbile, Jade – you havvd got a code!' He blew his nose for the hundredth time and gave a gloomy sniff. 'I wish I was biles frob everywhere! Sobewhere *I* could have sobe fud. Hullo, whad's that?' he said, staring, as a small dark shape leapt on to the sill.

73

'What's what?' she murmured dreamily.

'John! Barbara! And you too, Jane! Take off your coats at once. I will not have supper with Three Drowned Rats!' said Mary Poppins sharply.

They slithered off the window-seat and hurried to obey her. When Mary Poppins looked like that it was always best to obey.

The dark shape crept along the sill and a speckled face peeped in. Could it be – yes, it was! – a cat. A tortoiseshell cat with yellow eyes and a collar made of gold.

Michael pressed his nose to the pane. And the cat pressed its nose to the other side and looked at him thoughtfully. Then it smiled a most mysterious smile and, whisking off the window-sill, it sprang across Miss Lark's garden and disappeared over the roof.

'Who owns it, I wonder?' Michael murmured, as he gazed at the spot where the cat had vanished. He knew it couldn't belong to Miss Lark. She only cared for dogs.

'What are you looking at?' called Jane, as she dried her hair by the fire.

'Dothing!' he said in a horrid voice. He was not going to share the cat with her. She had had enough fun in the Park.

'I only asked,' she protested mildly.

He knew she was trying to be kind and something inside him wanted to melt. But his crossness would not let it.

'Ad I odly adswered!' he retorted.

Mary Poppins looked at him. He knew that look and he guessed what was coming, but he felt too tired to care.

'You,' she remarked in a chilly voice, 'can answer questions in bed. Spit-spot and in you go – and kindly close the door!'

Her eyes bored into him like gimlets as he stalked away to the night nursery and kicked the door to with a bang.

The steam-kettle bubbled beside his bed, sending out

fragrant whiffs of balsam. But he turned his nose away on purpose and put his head under the blankets.

'Dothing dice ever happeds to be,' he grumbled to his pillow.

But it offered its cool white cheek in silence as if it had not heard.

He gave it a couple of furious thumps, burrowed in like an angry rabbit, and immediately fell asleep.

A moment later – or so it seemed – he woke to find the morning sun streaming in upon him.

'What day is today, Mary Poppins?' he shouted.

'Thursday,' she called from the next room. Her voice, he thought, was strangely polite.

The camp-bed groaned as she sprang out. He could always tell what she was doing simply by the sound – the clip-clip of hooks and eyes, the swish of the hairbrush, the thump of her shoes and the rattle of the starched apron as she buttoned it round her waist. Then came a moment of solemn silence as she glanced approvingly at the mirror. And after that a hurricane as she whisked the others out of bed.

'May I get up, too, Mary Poppins?'

She answered 'Yes!', to his surprise, and he scrambled out like lightning in case she should change her mind.

His new sweater – navy blue with three red fir-trees – was lying on the chair. And for fear she would stop him wearing it, he dragged it quickly over his head and swaggered in to breakfast.

Jane was buttering her toast.

'How's your cold?' she inquired.

He gave an experimental sniff.

'Gone!' He seized the milk jug.

'I knew it would go,' she said, smiling. 'That's what I wished on the star last night.'

'Just as well you did,' he remarked. 'Now you've got me to play with.'

'There are always the Twins,' she reminded him.

'Not the same thing at all,' he said. 'May I have some more sugar, Mary Poppins?'

He fully expected her to say 'No!' But, instead, she smiled serenely.

'If you want it, Michael,' she replied, with the ladylike nod she reserved for strangers.

Could he believe his ears? he wondered. He hurriedly emptied the sugar bowl in case they had made a mistake.

'The post has come!' cried Mrs Banks, bustling in with a package. 'Nothing for anyone but Michael!'

He tore apart the paper and string. Aunt Flossie had sent him a cake of chocolate!

'Nut milk – my favourite!' he exclaimed, and was just about to take a bite when there came a knock at the door.

Robertson Ay shuffled slowly in.

'Message from Mrs Brill,' he yawned. 'She mixed a sponge cake, she says, and would like him to scrape the bowl!' He pointed a weary finger at Michael.

Scrape the cake-bowl! What a treat! And as rare as unexpected!

'I'm coming right away!' he shouted, stuffing the chocolate into his pocket. And, feeling rather bold and daring, he decided to slide down the banisters.

'The very chap I wanted to see!' cried Mr Banks, as Michael landed. He fumbled in his waistcoat pocket and handed his son a shilling.

'What's that for?' demanded Michael. He had never had a shilling before.

'To spend,' said Mr Banks solemnly, as he took his bowler hat and bag and hurried down the path.

Michael felt very proud and important. He puffed out his chest in a lordly way and clattered down to the kitchen.

'Good – is it, dearie?' said Mrs Brill, as he tasted the sticky substance.

'Delicious,' he said, smacking his lips.

But before he had time for another spoonful a well-known voice floated in from the Lane.

'All hands on deck! Up with the anchor! For I'm bound for the Rio Grande!'

It was Admiral Boom, setting out for a walk.

Upon his head was a black hat, painted with skull-and-crossbones – the one he had taken from a pirate chief in a desperate fight off Falmouth.

Away from the garden Michael dashed to get a look at it. For his dearest hope was that some day he, too, would have such a hat.

'Heave her over!' the Admiral roared, leaning against the front gate and lazily mopping his brow.

The autumn day was warm and misty. The sun was drawing into the sky the rain that had fallen last night.

'Blast my gizzard!' cried Admiral Boom, fanning himself with his hat. 'Tropical weather, that's what it is – it oughtn't to be allowed. The Admiral's hat is too hot for the Admiral. You take it, messmate, till I come back. For away I'm bound to go – oho! – 'cross the wide Missouri!'

And spreading his handkerchief over his head, he thrust the pirate's hat at Michael and stamped away, singing.

Michael clasped the skull-and-crossbones. His heart hammered with excitement as he put the hat on his head.

'I'll just go down the Lane,' he said, hoping that everybody in it would see him wearing the treasure. It banged against his brow as he walked and wobbled whenever he looked up. But nevertheless, behind each curtain – he was sure – there lurked an admiring eye.

It was not until he was nearly home that he noticed Miss Lark's dogs. They had thrust their heads through the garden fence and were looking at him in astonishment.

Andrew's tail gave a well-bred wag, but Willoughby merely stared.

'Luncheon!' trilled Miss Lark's voice.

And as Willoughby rose to answer the summons he winked at Andrew and sniggered.

'Can he be laughing at me?' thought Michael. But he put the idea aside as ridiculous and sauntered up to the nursery.

'Do I have to wash my hands, Mary Poppins? They're quite clean,' he assured her.

'Well, the others, of course, have washed theirs – but you do as *you* think best!'

At last she realized, he thought, that Michael Banks was no ordinary boy. He could wash or not, as *he* thought best, and she hadn't even told him to take off his hat! He decided to go straight in to luncheon.

'Now, away to the Park,' said Mary Poppins, as soon as the meal was over. 'If that is convenient for *you*, Michael?' She waited for his approval.

'Oh, perfickly convenient!' He gave a lordly wave of his hand. 'I think I shall go to the swings.'

'Not to the Lake?' protested Jane. She wanted to look at Neleus.

'Certainly not!' said Mary Poppins. 'We shall do what Michael wishes!'

And she stood aside respectfully as he strutted before her through the gate.

The soft bright mist still rose from the grass, blurring the shapes of seats and fountains. Bushes and trees seemed to float in the air. Nothing was like its real self until you were close upon it.

Mary Poppins sat down on a bench, settled the perambulator beside her and began to read a book. The children dashed away to the playground.

Up and down on the swings went Michael, with the pirate's hat bumping against his eyes. Then he took a ride on the spinning-jenny and after that, the loop. He couldn't turn somersaults, like Jane, for fear of dropping the hat.

'What next?' he thought, feeling rather bored. Everything possible, he felt, had happened to him this morning. Now there was nothing left to do.

He wandered back through the weaving mist and sat beside Mary Poppins. She gave him a small, preoccupied smile, as though she had never seen him before, and went on reading her book. It was called *Everything a Lady Should Know*.

Michael sighed to attract her attention.

But she did not seem to hear.

He kicked a hole in the rainy grass.

Mary Poppins read on

Then his eye fell on her open handbag which was lying on the seat. Inside it was a handkerchief, and beneath the handkerchief a mirror and beside the mirror her silver whistle.

He gazed at it with envious eyes. Then he glanced at Mary Poppins. There she was, still deep in her book. Should he ask her again for a loan of the whistle? She seemed to be in the best of humours – not a cross word the whole day long.

79

But was the humour to be relied on? Suppose he asked and she said no!

He decided not to risk asking, but just to take the whistle. It was only borrowing, after all. He could put it back in a minute.

Quick as a fish his hand darted, and the whistle was in his trouser pocket.

Round behind the bench he hurried, feeling the silver shape against him. He was just about to take it out when something small and bright ran past him.

'I believe that's the cat I saw last night!' said Michael to himself.

And, indeed, it was one and the same. The same black-and-yellow coat shone in the sunny mist, more like dapples of light and shadow than ordinary fur. And about its neck was the same gold collar.

The cat glanced up invitingly, smiling the same mysterious smile, and padded lightly on.

Michael darted after it, in and out of the patches of mist that seemed to grow thicker as he ran.

Something fell with a chink at his feet.

'My shilling!' he cried, as he bent to retrieve it. He searched among the steaming grasses, turning over the wet blades, feeling under the clover. Not here! Not there! Where could it have gone?

'Come on!' said a soft, inviting voice. He looked round quickly. To his surprise there was nobody near – except the smiling cat.

'Hurry!' cried the voice again.

It was the cat who had spoken.

Michael sprang up. It was no use hunting, the shilling had gone. He hurried after the voice.

The cat smiled as he caught it up and rubbed against his legs. The steaming vapour rose up from the earth, wrapping them both around. And before them stood a wall of mist almost as thick as a cloud.

'Take hold of my collar,' the cat advised. Its voice was no more than a soft mew, but it held a note of command.

Michael felt a twinge of excitement. Something new was happening! He bent down obediently and clasped the band of gold.

'Now, jump!' the cat ordered. 'Lift your feet!'

And holding the golden collar tightly, Michael sprang into the mist.

'Whee – ee – ee!' cried a rushing wind in his ears. The sunny cloud was sweeping past him and all around him was empty space. The only solid things in the world were the shining band round the cat's neck and the hat on his own head.

'Where on earth are we going?' Michael gasped.

At the same moment the mist cleared. His feet touched something firm and shiny. And he saw that he stood on the steps of a palace – a palace made of gold.

'Nowhere on earth,' replied the cat, pressing a bell with its paw.

The doors of the palace opened slowly. Sweet music came to Michael's ears and the sight he beheld quite dazzled him.

Before him lay a great gold hall, blazing with plumes of light. Never, in his richest dreams, had Michael imagined such splendour. But the grandeur of the palace was as nothing compared to the brilliance of its inhabitants. For the hall was full of cats.

There were cats playing fiddles, cats playing flutes, cats on trapezes, cats in hammocks; cats juggling with golden hoops, cats dancing on the tips of their toes; cats turning somersaults; cats chasing tails and cats merely lolling about daintily licking their paws.

Moreover, they were tortoiseshell cats, all of them dappled with yellow and black; and the light in the hall seemed to come from their coats, for each cat shone with its own brightness.

In the centre, before a golden curtain, lay a pair of golden cushions. And on these reclined two dazzling creatures, each wearing a crown of gold. They leaned together, paw in paw, majestically surveying the scene.

'They must be the King and Queen,' thought Michael.

To one side of this lordly pair stood three very young cats. Their fur was as smooth and bright as sunlight, and each had a chaplet of yellow flowers perched between the ears. Round about them were other cats who looked like courtiers – for all were wearing golden collars and ceremoniously standing on their hind legs.

One of these turned and beckoned to Michael.

'Here he is, Your Majesty!' He bowed obsequiously.

'Ah,' said the King, with a stately nod. 'So glad you've turned up at last! The Queen and I and our three daughters' – he waved his paw at the three young cats – 'have been expecting you!'

Expecting him! How flattering! But, of course, no more than his due.

'May we offer you a little refreshment?' asked the Queen, with a gracious smile.

'Yes, please!' said Michael eagerly. In such a graceful environment there would surely be nothing less than jelly – and probably ice-cream!

Immediately three courtier cats presented three golden platters. On one lay a dead mouse, on the second a bat, and the third held a small raw fish.

Michael felt his face fall. 'Oh no! thank you!' he said, with a shudder.

'First Yes Please and then No Thank You! Which do you mean?' the King demanded.

'Well, I don't like mice!' protested Michael. 'And I never eat bats or raw fish either.'

'Don't like mice?' cried a hundred voices, as the cats all stared at each other.

'Fancy!' exclaimed the three Princesses.

'Then perhaps you would care for a little milk?' said the Queen, with a queenly smile.

At once a courtier stood before him with milk in a golden saucer.

Michael put out his hands to take it.

'Oh, not with your paws!' the Queen implored him. 'Let him hold it while you lap!'

'But I *can't* lap!' Michael protested. 'I haven't got that kind of tongue.'

'Can't lap!' Again the cats regarded each other. They seemed quite scandalized.

'Fancy!' the three Princesses mewed.

'Well,' said the Queen hospitably, 'a little rest after your journey!'

'Oh, it wasn't much of a journey,' said Michael. 'Just a big jump and here we were! It's funny,' he went on, thoughtfully, 'I've never seen this palace before – and I'm always in the Park! It must have been hidden behind the trees.'

'In the Park?'

The King and Queen raised their eyebrows. So did all the courtiers. And the three Princesses were so overcome that they took three golden fans from their pockets and hid their smiles behind them.

'You're not in the Park now, I assure you. Far from it!' the King informed him.

'Well, it can't be *very* far,' said Michael. 'It only took me a minute to get here.'

'Ah!' said the King. 'But how long is a minute?'

'Sixty seconds!' Michael replied. Surely, he thought, a King should know that!

'*Your* minutes may be sixty seconds, but ours are about two hundred years.'

Michael smiled at him amiably. A King, he thought, must have his joke.

'Now tell me,' continued the King blandly, 'did you ever hear of the Dog Star?'

'Yes,' said Michael, very surprised. What had the Dog Star to do with it? 'His other name is Sirius.'

'Well, this,' said the King, 'is the Cat Star. And its other name is a secret. A secret, may I further add, that is only known to cats.'

'But how did I get here?' Michael inquired. He was feeling more and more pleased with himself. Think of it – visiting a star! That didn't happen to everyone.

'You wished,' replied the King calmly.

'Did I?' He couldn't remember it.

'Of course you did!' the King retorted.

'Last night!' the Queen reminded him.

'Looking at the first star!' the courtiers added firmly.

'Which happened,' said the King, 'to be ours. Read the Report, Lord Chamberlain!'

An elderly cat, in spectacles and a long gold wig, stepped forward with an enormous book.

'Last night,' he read out pompously, 'Michael Banks, of Number Seventeen, Cherry Tree Lane – a little house on the planet Earth – gave expression to three wishes.'

'Three?' cried Michael. 'I never did!'

'Shush!' warned the King. 'Don't interrupt.'

'Wish Number One,' the Lord Chamberlain read, 'was that *he* could have some luck!'

A memory stirred in Michael's mind. He saw himself on the window-seat, gazing up at the sky.

'Oh, now I remember!' he agreed. 'But it wasn't very important.'

'All wishes are important!' The Lord Chamberlain looked at him severely.

An elderly cat stepped forward

'Well – and what happened?' the King inquired. 'I presume the wish came true?'

Michael reflected. It had been a most unusual day, full of all kinds of luck.

'Yes, it did!' he admitted cheerfully.

'In what way?' asked the King. 'Do tell us!'

'Well,' began Michael, 'I scraped the cake bowl –'

'Scraped the cake bowl?' the cats repeated. They stared as though he were out of his wits.

'Fancy!' the three Princesses purred.

The King wrinkled his nose in disgust. 'Some people have strange ideas of luck! But do continue, please!'

Michael straightened his shoulders proudly. 'And then – because it was hot, you know – the Admiral let me borrow this hat!' What would they say to that? he wondered. They would surely be green with envy.

But the cats merely flicked their tails and silently gazed at the skull-and-crossbones.

'Well, everyone to his own taste,' said the King after a pause. 'The question is – is it comfortable?'

'Er – not exactly,' Michael admitted. For the hat did not fit him anywhere. 'It's rather heavy,' he added.

'H'm!' the King murmured. 'Well, please go on!'

'Then Daddy gave me a shilling this morning. But I lost it in the grass.'

'How much use is a lost shilling?' The way the King put the question, it sounded like a conundrum.

Michael wished he had been more careful.

'Not much,' he said. Then he brightened up.

'Oh – and Aunt Flossie sent me a bar of chocolate.'

He felt for it in his trouser pocket and realized, as he fished it out, that he must have been sitting on it. For now it was only a flattened mass with bits of fluff all over it and a nail embedded among the nuts.

The cats eyed the object fastidiously.

'If you ask me,' said the King, looking squeamish, 'I much prefer a bat to that!'

Michael also stared at the chocolate. How quickly all his luck had vanished! There was nothing left to show for it.

'Read on, Lord Chamberlain!' ordered the King.

The old cat gave his wig a pat.

'The second wish was' – he turned the page – 'that the others would leave him alone.'

'It wasn't!' cried Michael uncomfortably.

But he saw himself, even as he spoke, pushing the Twins away.

'Well,' he said lamely, 'perhaps it was. But I didn't really mean it!'

The King straightened up on his golden cushion.

'You made a wish that you didn't mean? Wasn't that rather dangerous?'

'And *did* they leave you alone?' asked the Queen. Her eyes were very inquisitive.

Michael considered. Now that he came to think of it, in spite of his luck, the day had been lonely. Jane had played her own games. The Twins had hardly been near him. And Mary Poppins, although she had treated him most politely, had certainly left him alone.

'Yes,' he admitted unwillingly.

'Of course they did!' the King declared. 'If you wish on the first star, it always comes true, especially' – he twirled his whiskers – 'if it happens to be ours. Well, what about the third wish?'

The Lord Chamberlain adjusted his glasses.

'He wished to be miles from everybody and somewhere where *he* could have all the fun.'

'But that was only a sort of joke! I didn't even realize I was looking at a star. And I never thought of it coming true.'

'Exactly so! You never thought! That's what all of them say.' The King regarded him quizzically.

'All?' echoed Michael. 'Who else said it?'

'Dear me!' The King gave a dainty yawn. 'You don't think you're the only child who has wished to be miles away! I assure you, it's quite a common request. And one – when it's wished on *our* star – that *we* find very useful. *Very useful indeed!*' he repeated. 'Malkin!' He waved to a courtier. 'Be good enough to draw the curtain!'

A young cat, whom Michael recognized as the one that had accompanied him from the Park, sprang to the back of the hall.

The golden curtain swung aside, disclosing the palace kitchens.

'Now, come along!' cried Malkin sternly. 'Hurry up, all! No dawdling!'

'Yes, Malkin!'

'No, Malkin!'

'Coming, Malkin!'

A chorus of treble voices answered. And Michael saw, to his surprise, that the kitchen was full of children.

There were boys and girls of every size, all of them working frantically at different domestic tasks.

Some were washing up golden plates, others were shining the cats' gold collars. One boy was skinning mice, another was boning bats, and two more were down on their knees busily scrubbing the floor. Two little girls in party dresses were sweeping up fishbones and sardine tins and putting them into a golden dustbin. Another was sitting under a table winding a skein of golden wool. They all looked very forlorn and harassed, and the child beneath the table was weeping.

The Lord Chamberlain looked at her and gave an impatient growl.

'Be quick with that wool, now, Arabella! The Princesses want to play cat's-cradle!'

The Queen stretched out her hind leg to a boy in a sailor suit.

'Come, Robert,' she said in a fretful voice. 'It's time to polish my claws.'

'I'm hungry!' whined the eldest Princess.

'Matilda! Matilda!' Malkin thundered. 'A haddock for Princess Tiger-Lily! And Princess Marigold's sugared milk! And a rat for the Princess Crocus!'

A girl in plaits and a pinafore appeared with three golden bowls. The Princesses nibbled a morsel each and tossed the rest to the floor. And several children ran in and began to sweep up the scraps.

The King glanced slyly across at Michael and smiled at his astonishment.

'Our servants are very well trained, don't you think? Malkin insists on them toeing the line. They keep the

palace like a new pin. And they cost us practically nothing.'

'But —' began Michael in a very small voice. 'Do the children do all the work?'

'Who else?' said the King, with the lift of an eyebrow. 'You could hardly expect a cat to do it! Cats have other and better occupations. A cat in the kitchen — what an idea! Our duty is to be wise and handsome — isn't that enough?'

Michael's face was full of pity as he gazed at the luckless children.

'But how did they get here?' he wanted to know.

'Exactly as you did,' the King replied. 'They wished they were miles from everywhere. So here they are, you see.'

'But that wasn't what they really wanted!'

'I'm afraid that's no affair of ours. All we can do is to

grant their wishes. I'll introduce you in a moment. They're always glad to see a new face. And so are we, for that matter.' The King's face wore an expressive smile. 'Many hands make light work, you know!'

'But *I'm* not going to work!' cried Michael. 'That wasn't what I wished for.'

'Ah! Then you should have been more careful. Wishes are tricky things. You must ask for *exactly* what you want or you never know where they will land you. Well, never mind. You'll soon settle down.'

'Settle down?' echoed Michael uneasily.

'Certainly. Just as the others have done. Malkin will show you your duties presently, when you've had the rest of your wish. We mustn't be forgetting that. There are still the riddles, you know.'

'Riddles? I never mentioned riddles!' Michael was beginning to wonder if he were really enjoying this adventure.

'Didn't you wish to have all the fun? Well, what is more fun than a riddle? Especially,' purred the King, 'to a cat! Tell him the rules, Lord Chamberlain!'

The old cat peered over his glasses.

'It has always been our custom here, when any child wishes for all the fun to let him have three guesses. If he answers them all – correctly, of course – he wins a third of the Cats' kingdom and the hand of one of the Princesses in marriage.'

'And if he fails,' the King added, 'we find him *some other occupation*.' He glanced significantly at the labouring children.

'I need hardly add,' he continued blandly, exchanging a smile with his three daughters, 'that no one has guessed the riddles yet. Let the curtain be drawn for the – ahem! – time being. Silence in the hall, please! Lord Chamberlain, begin!'

Immediately, the music ceased. The dancers stood on the tips of their paws and the hoops hung motionless in the air.

Michael's spirits rose again. Now that the children were out of sight, he felt a good deal better. Besides, he loved a guessing game.

The Lord Chamberlain opened his book and read:

'Round as a marble, blue as the sea,
Unless I am brown or grey, maybe!
Smile, and I shine my window-pane,
Frown at me and down comes my rain.
I see all things but nothing I hear,
Sing me to sleep and I disappear.'

Michael frowned. The cats were all watching him as if he were a mouse.

'A bit of a poser, I'm afraid!' The King leaned back on his cushion.

'No, it isn't!' cried Michael suddenly. 'I've got it! An Eye!'

The cats glanced cornerwise at each other. The King's wide gaze grew narrower.

'H'm,' he murmured. 'Not bad, not bad! Well, now for the second riddle.'

'A-hurrrrrum!' The Lord Chamberlain cleared his throat.

'Deep within me is a bird
And in that bird another me,
And in that me a bird again –
Now what am I, in letters three?'

'That's easy!' Michael gave a shout. 'The answer's an Egg, of course!'

Again the cats swivelled their eyes.

'You are right,' said the King unwillingly. He seemed

to be only faintly pleased. 'But I wonder' – he arched his dappled back – 'I wonder what you will make of the third!'

'Silence!' commanded the Lord Chamberlain, though there wasn't a sound in the hall.

> 'Elegant the jungle beast
> That lives in field and fold.
> He's like the sun when he is young
> And like the moon when old.
> He sees no clock, he hears no chime
> And yet he always knows the time.'

'This is more difficult,' Michael murmured. 'The third is always the worst. H'm, let me see – a jungle beast – he's elegant and he knows the time. Oh, dear, it's on the tip of my tongue. I've got it! Dandelion!'

'He's guessed it!' cried the King, rising.

And at once the cats all leapt to life. They surrounded Michael with fur and whiskers and arched themselves against him.

'You are cleverer than I thought,' said the King. 'Almost as clever as a cat. Well, now I must go and divide the kingdom. And as to a bride – the Princess Crocus, it seems to me, would be the most suitable choice.'

'Oh, thank you,' said Michael cheerfully – he was feeling quite himself again – 'but I must be getting home now.'

'Home!' cried the King in astonishment.

'Home?' the Queen echoed, raising her eyebrows.

'Well, I have to be back for tea,' explained Michael.

'Tea?' repeated the courtiers, gaping.

'Fancy!' the three Princesses tittered.

'Are you so certain you still have a home?' said the King in a curious voice.

'Of course I am,' said Michael, staring. 'What could

have happened to it? From the Park to – er – here, it was just a jump. And it only took me a minute.'

'You've forgotten, I think,' said the King smoothly, 'that our minutes last for two hundred years. And as you've been here at least half an hour –'

'Two hundred?' Michael's cheek paled. So it hadn't been a joke after all!

'It stands to reason,' the King continued, 'that many changes must have occurred since you were on the Earth. Number Seventeen Apple-bush Avenue –'

'Cherry Tree Lane,' the Lord Chamberlain muttered.

'Well, whatever its name, you may be sure it isn't the same as it was. I dare say it's overgrown with brambles –'

'Briars!' added the Queen, purring.

'Nettles,' suggested the courtiers.

'Blackberries,' murmured the three Princesses.

'Oh, I'm sure it isn't!' Michael gulped. He was feeling such a longing for home that the thought of it made him choke.

'However,' the King went blandly on, 'if you're certain you can find your way – I'm afraid we can't spare Malkin again – by all means set out!' He waved his paw towards the door.

Michael ran to the entrance. 'Of course I'm certain!' he cried stoutly. But his courage ebbed as he looked out.

There were the shining steps of the palace, but below them, as far as he could see, there was nothing but wreathing mist. What if he jumped? he thought to himself. And if he jumped, where would he land?

He bit his lip and turned back to the hall. The cats were softly creeping towards him, gazing at him mockingly from black-and-yellow eyes.

'You see!' said the King of the Cats, smiling – and not a kindly smile either. 'In spite of being so clever at guessing, you do not know the way back! You wished to be miles from everywhere, but you foolishly neglected to add that you would also like to return home. Well! Well! Everyone makes mistakes at times – unless, of course, they are cats! And think how fortunate you are! No kitchen work – you have solved the riddles. Plenty of rats and bats and spiders. And you can settle down with the Princess Crocus and live happily ever after.'

'But I don't *want* to marry the Princess Crocus! I only want to go home!'

A low growl came from every throat. Every whisker bristled.

'You ... don't ... want ... to ... marry ... the ... Princess ... Crocus?'

Word by word the King came nearer, growing larger at every step.

'No I don't!' declared Michael. 'She's only a cat!'

'*Only* a cat!' the cats squealed, swelling and rearing with rage.

Black-and-yellow shapes swarmed round him. '*Only* a cat!' They spat out the words.

'Oh, what shall I do?' He backed away, shielding his eyes from their gaze.

'You wissshed!' they hissed at him, padding closer. 'You sssought our ssstar! You mussst take the conssssequen-cesss!'

'Oh, where shall I go?' cried Michael wildly.

'You will ssstay bessside usss,' the King whispered with a terrible cat-like softness. 'You guesssed our riddlesss, you ssstole our sssecretsss. Do you think we would let you go?'

A wall of cats was all about him. He flung out an arm to thrust it away. But their arching backs were too much for him. His hand dropped limply to his side and fell upon the rigid shape of Mary Poppins' whistle.

With a cry, he snatched it from his pocket and blew it with all his might.

A shrill peal sounded through the Hall.

'Sssilence him! Ssseize him! He mussstn't essscape!'

The furious cats pressed closer.

In desperation he blew again.

A whining caterwaul answered the blast as a wave of cats rolled forward.

He felt himself enveloped in fur – fur in his nose, fur in his eyes. Oh, which of them had leapt at him – or was it all the cats together? With their screeches echoing in his ears, he felt himself borne upwards. A fur-covered arm, or perhaps a leg, was clasped about his waist. And his face was crushed to a furry something – a breast or a back, he could not tell.

Wind was blowing everywhere, sweeping him wildly on, with cat to the right of him, cat to the left of him, cat above him and cat below. He was wrapped in a cocoon of cats and the long furry arm that held him was as strong as an iron band.

With an effort he wrenched his head sideways and blew the whistle so violently that his hat fell off his head.

The strong arm drew him closer still.

'Whee – ee!' cried the wind, with a hollow voice.

And now it seemed that he and the cats were falling through the air. Down, down, down in a furry mass. Oh, where were they taking him?

Again and again he blew the whistle, struggling madly against the fur and kicking in all directions.

'Oo's making all that dreadful rumpus? Mind what you're doin'! You knocked off me cap!'

A wonderfully familiar voice sounded in Michael's ears.

Cautiously he opened an eye and saw that he was drifting down past the top of a chestnut-tree.

The next minute his feet touched the dewy grass

The next minute his feet touched the dewy grass of the Park and there, on the lawn, was the Park Keeper, looking as though he had seen a ghost.

'Now, now! Wot's all this. Wot 'ave you two been up to?'

You *two*! The words had a cheerful ring. He was held, it seemed, by only one cat and not, after all, by the whole tribe. Was it the Lord Chamberlain? Or, perhaps, the Princess Crocus!'

Michael glanced from the Park Keeper to the furry arm around him. It ended, to his great surprise, not in a paw – but a hand. And on the hand was a neat glove – black, not tortoiseshell.

He turned his head inquiringly and his cheek encountered a bone button that was nestling in the fur. Surely he knew that piece of bone! Oh, was it possible –? Could it be –?

His glance slid upwards past the button till it came to a neat fur collar. And above the collar was a circle of straw topped with a crimson flower.

He gave a long-drawn sigh of relief. Cats, he was glad to realize, do not wear tulip hats on their heads, nor kid gloves over their claws.

'It's you!' he cried exultantly, pressing his face to her rabbit-skin jacket. 'Oh, Mary Poppins – I was up in the star – and all the cats came snarling at me – and I thought I'd never find the way home – and I blew the whistle, and –'

Suddenly he began to stammer, for her face, beneath the brim of her hat, was cold and very haughty.

'And here I am –' he concluded lamely.

Mary Poppins said never a word. She bowed to him in a distant manner as though she had never met him before. Then in silence she held out her hand.

He hung his head guiltily and put the whistle into it.

'So *that's* the reason for the hullabaloo!' The Park Keeper spluttered with disapproval. 'I warn you, this is your last chance. Blow that whistle once again and I'll resign – I promise!'

'A pie-crust promise!' scoffed Mary Poppins, as she pocketed the whistle.

The Park Keeper shook his head in despair.

'You ought to know the rules by now. All litter to be placed in the baskets. No climbin' of trees in the Park!'

'Litter yourself!' said Mary Poppins. 'And I never climbed a tree in my life!'

'Well, might I inquire where you came from, then? Droppin' down from the sky like that and knockin' off me cap?'

'There's not a law against inquiring, so far as I am aware!'

'Been up in the Milky Way, I suppose!' The Park Keeper snorted sarcastically.

'Exactly,' she said, with a smile of triumph.

'Huh! You can't expect me – a respectable man – to believe that tarradiddle!' And yet, he thought uneasily, she had certainly come from somewhere.

'I don't expect anything,' she retorted. 'And I'll thank you to let me pass!'

Still holding Michael close to her side, she gave her head a disdainful toss, pushed the Park Keeper out of the way and tripped towards the Gate.

An outraged cry sounded behind them as the Park Keeper wildly waved his stick.

'You've broken the rules! You've disturbed the peace! And you don't even say you're sorry!'

'I'm not!' she called back airily, as she whisked across the Lane.

Speechless at so many broken bye-laws, the Park Keeper bent to pick up his cap. There it lay on the rainy grass.

And beside it sprawled a strange dark object on which was painted, in gleaming white, a design of skull-and-cross-bones.

'When will they learn,' he sighed to himself, 'what to do with their litter?'

And because he was so upset and flustered, he mistakenly put his cap in the basket and walked home wearing the pirate's hat . . .

Michael glanced eagerly at Number Seventeen as they hurried across the Lane. It was easy to see – for the mist had cleared – that there wasn't a bramble near it. The cats had not been right, after all.

The hall light flooded him with welcome and the stairs seemed to run away beneath him as he bounded up to the nursery.

'Oh, there you are,' cried Jane gaily. 'Wherever have you been?'

He had not the words to answer her. He could only gaze at the well-known room, as though he had been away for years. How could he explain, even to Jane, how precious it seemed to him?

The Twins ran in with open arms. He bent and hugged them lovingly and, putting out his hand to Jane, he drew her into the hug.

A light footstep made him glance up. Mary Poppins came tripping in, buttoning on her apron. Everything about her tonight – the darting movements, the stern glance, even the way her nose turned up – was deliciously familiar.

'What would you like me to do, Mary Poppins?' He hoped she would ask for something tremendous.

'Whatever *you* like,' she answered calmly, with the same extravagant courtesy she had shown him all day long.

'Don't, Mary Poppins! Don't!' he pleaded.

'Don't what?' she inquired, with annoying calm.

'Don't speak to me in that elegant way. I can't bear any more luck!'

'But luck,' she said brightly, 'was what you wanted!'

'It was. But it isn't. I've had enough. Oh, don't be polite and kind.'

The cool smile faded from her face.

'And am I not usually polite? Have you ever known me to be unkind? What do you take me for – a hyena?'

'No, not a hyena, Mary Poppins. And you *are* polite and you *are* kind! But today I like you best when you're angry. It makes me feel much safer.'

'Indeed? And when am I angry, I'd like to know?'

She looked, as she spoke, very angry indeed. Her eyes flashed, her cheeks were scarlet. And for once, the sight delighted him. Now that her chilly smile was gone, he didn't mind what happened. She was her own familiar self and he no longer a stranger.

'And when you sniff – that's when I like you!' he added with stupendous daring.

'Sniff?' she said, sniffing. 'What an idea!'

'And when you say "Humph" – like a camel!'

'Like a what?' She looked quite petrified. Then she bristled wrathfully. She reminded him of the wave of cats as she crossed the nursery like an oncoming storm.

'You dare to stand there,' she accused him sternly, taking a step with every word, just as the King had done, 'and tell me I'm a dromedary? Four legs and a tail and a hump or two?'

'But, Mary Poppins, I only meant –'

'That is enough from you, Michael. One more piece of impertinence and you'll go to bed, spit-spot.'

'I'm in it already, Mary Poppins,' he said in a quavering voice. For by now she had backed him through the nursery into his room and on to his bed.

'First a hyena and then a camel. I suppose I'll be a gorilla next!'

'But –'

'Not another word!' she spluttered, giving her head a proud toss as she stalked out of the room.

He knew he had insulted her, but he couldn't really be sorry. She was so exactly like herself that all he could feel was gladness.

Off went his clothes and in he dived, hugging his pillow to him. Its cheek was warm and friendly now as it pressed against his own.

The shadows crept slowly across his bed as he listened to the familiar sounds – bath-water running, the Twins' chatter and the rattle and clink of nursery supper.

The sounds grew fainter . . . the pillow grew softer . . .

But, suddenly, a delicious something – a scent or a fla-

vour – filled the room, and made him sit up with a start.

A cup of chocolate hovered above him. Its fragrance came sweetly to his nose and mingled with the fresh-toast scent of Mary Poppins' apron. There she stood, like a starched statue, gazing calmly down.

He met her glance contentedly, feeling it plunging into him and seeing what was there. He knew that she knew that he knew she was not a camel. The day was over, his adventure behind him. The Cat Star was far away in the sky. And it seemed to him, as he stirred his chocolate, he had everything he wanted.

'I do believe, Mary Poppins,' he said, 'that I've nothing left to wish for.'

She smiled a superior, sceptical smile.

'Humph!' she remarked. 'That's lucky!'

CHAPTER FOUR

The Children in the Story

Rattle! Rattle! Rattle!

Clank! Clank! Clank!

Up and down went the lawn-mower, leaving stripes of newly-cut grass in its wake.

Behind it panted the Park Keeper, pushing with all his might. At the end of each stripe he paused for a moment to glance round the Park and make sure that everybody was observing the rules.

Suddenly, out of the corner of his eye, he spied a large net waving backwards and forwards behind the laurels.

'Benjamin!' he called warningly. 'Benjamin Winkle, remember the bye-laws!'

The Keeper of the Zoological Gardens thrust his head round a clump of leaves and put his finger to his lips. He was a small, nervous-looking man, with a beard like a ham-frill fringing his face.

'Sh!' he whispered. 'I'm after an Admiral!'

'A Nadmiral? Well, you won't find 'im in a laurel bush. 'E's over there, at the end of the Lane. Big 'ouse, with a telescope on the flagpole.'

'I mean a *Red* Admiral!' hissed the Keeper of the Zoological Gardens.

'Well, '*e's* red enough for anything. Got a face like a stormy sunset!'

'It's not a man I'm after, Fred.' The Keeper of the

Zoological Gardens gave the Park Keeper a look of solemn reproach. 'I'm catching butterflies for the Insect House, and all I've got' – he glanced dejectedly into his net – 'is one Cabbage White.'

'Cabbage?' cried the Park Keeper, rattling off down the lawn. 'If you want a cabbage, I've some in my garden. H'artichokes, too. And turnips! Fine day, Egbert!' he called to the Policeman, who was taking a short-cut through the Park, in the course of his daily duties.

'Might be worse,' the Policeman agreed, glancing up at the windows of Number Seventeen, in the hope of catching a glimpse of Ellen.

He sighed. 'And might be better!' he added glumly. For Ellen was nowhere to be seen.

Rattle, rattle! Clank, clank!

The sunlight spangled the stripy lawn and spread like a fan over Park and Lane. It even went so far as to shine on the Fair Ground, and the swinging-boats and the merry-go-round and the big blue banner with MUDGE'S FAIR printed on it in gold.

The Park Keeper paused at the end of a stripe and sent a hawk-like glance about him.

A fat man with a face like a poppy was sauntering through the little gate that led from the Fair. He had a bowler hat on the back of his head and a large cigar in his mouth.

'Keep Off the Grass!' the Park Keeper called to him.

'I wasn't on it!' retorted the fat man, with a look of injured innocence.

'Well, I'm just givin' you a Word of Warnin'. All litter to be placed in the baskets – especially, Mr Mudge, in the Fair Ground!'

'Mr Smith,' said the fat man in a fat, confident voice, 'if you find so much as a postage stamp when the Fair's over, I'll – well I'll be surprised. You'll be able to eat your dinner off that Fair Ground, or my name's not Willie Mudge.'

And he stuck his thumbs into the armholes of his jacket and swaggered off, looking very important.

'Last year,' the Park Keeper shouted after him, 'I swept up sacks of postage stamps! And I don't eat me dinner there. I go 'ome for it!'

He turned to his work again with a sigh and the lawn-mower went up and down with a steady, sleepy drone. At the last stripe, where the lawn ended in the Rose Garden, he glanced cautiously round. Now was the moment, he felt, if there was nobody about to report him to the Lord Mayor, to take a little rest.

The Rose Garden was a ring of rose-beds enclosing a little green space. In the middle was a pool, and in the pool stood a fountain of white marble shaped like an open rose.

The Park Keeper peered through the flowering bushes. There, by the fountain, lay Jane and Michael. And just

beyond the Rose Garden, on a marble seat, sat an elderly gentleman. He seemed to have forgotten his hat, for his bald head was sheltered from the sun by a peaked cap made of newspaper. His nose was deep in an enormous book, which he was reading with the aid of a magnifying-glass. He muttered to himself as he turned the pages.

Jane and Michael, too, had a book. And Jane's voice mingled with the sound of the fountain as she read aloud to Michael. It was a peaceful scene.

'Quiet for once,' the Park Keeper murmured. 'I shall just snatch Forty Winks!' And he lay down cautiously among the bushes hoping that if anyone passed they would mistake him for a rose.

Had he looked in the other direction he might have thought better of behaving so recklessly. For, away under the wistarias, pushing the perambulator backwards and forwards in a rhythmic, soothing movement, was Mary Poppins.

Creak, creak, went the wheels.

Whimper, whimper, went Annabel, who was cutting her first tooth.

'Shoo now! Shoo now!' murmured Mary Poppins, in an absent-minded voice.

She was thinking about her new pink blouse, with the lace-edged handkerchief stuck in the pocket. How nicely it harmonized, she thought, with the tulip in her hat. And she could not help wishing there were more people in the Park to appreciate the spectacle. On every bench and under every tree there should have been an admiring onlooker. 'There's that charming Miss Poppins,' she imagined them saying, 'always so neat and respectable!'

But there were only a few scattered strangers hurrying along the paths and taking no notice of anybody.

She could see the Policeman forlornly gazing up at the windows of Number Seventeen. And the fat man with the large cigar who, in spite of all the Park Keeper's warnings, was walking on the grass. She prinked a little as Bert, the Match Man, biting into a rosy apple, came sauntering through the Gate. Perhaps he was looking for her, she thought, smoothing her neat black gloves.

She could also see Miss Lark, whose two dogs were taking her for an afternoon run. They rushed down the Long Walk laughing and barking, while Miss Lark, with the two leads in her hands, came tumbling behind. Her hat was over one ear and her scarf flapped about like a flag in the breeze. Gloves and spectacles scattered from her, and her necklaces and beads and bracelets were swinging in all directions.

Mary Poppins sniffed. Miss Lark, she thought, was not so tidy as *somebody* she could mention! She smiled a small self-satisfied smile and went on rocking Annabel.

Now that the lawn-mower was silent, there was hardly a sound in the Park. Only the music of the fountain and Jane's voice coming to the end of a story.

'So that,' she concluded, 'was the end of the Witch. And the King and the Maiden were married next day and lived happily ever after.'

Michael sighed contentedly and nibbled a leaf of clover.

Away beyond the Rose Garden, the elderly gentleman took off his glasses, spread his handkerchief over his face and dozed on the marble seat.

'Go on, Jane. Don't stop!' urged Michael. 'Read another one.'

Jane turned the pages of *The Silver Fairy Book*. It was worn and faded, for its life had been long and busy. Once it had belonged to Mrs Banks, and before that it had been given to her mother by *her* mother. Many of the pictures had disappeared and the drawings had all been coloured with crayons, either by Jane and Michael or by their mother. Perhaps, even, by their Grandmother, too.

'It's so hard to choose,' Jane murmured, for she loved every one of the stories.

'Well, read wherever it falls open – the way you always do!'

She closed the book, held it between her hands for a second, and then let it go. With a little thud it fell on the grass and opened right in the middle.

'Hooray!' said Michael. 'It's *The Three Princes*.' And he settled himself to listen.

'Once upon a time,' read Jane, 'there lived a King who had three sons. The eldest was Prince Florimond, the second Prince Veritain, and the third Prince Amor. Now, it so happened that –'

'Let me see the picture!' interrupted Michael.

It was a drawing he particularly liked, for he and Jane had coloured it one rainy afternoon. The Princes were standing at the edge of a forest and the branches that spread above their heads bore fruit and flowers together. A saddled Unicorn stood beside them, with its rein looped round the arm of the eldest.

Prince Florimond was in green crayon with a purple cap. Prince Veritain had an orange jerkin and his cap was scarlet. And little Prince Amor was all in blue, with a golden dagger stuck in his belt. Chrome-coloured ringlets fell about the shoulders of the two elder brothers. And the youngest, who was bareheaded, had a yellow circlet of short curls, rather like a crown.

As for the Unicorn, he was silvery white from mane to tail – except for his eyes, which were the colour of forget-me-nots; and his horn, which was striped with red and black.

Jane and Michael gazed down at the page and smiled at the pictured children. And the three Princes smiled up from the book and seemed to lean forward from the forest.

Michael sighed. 'If only I had a dagger like Amor's. It would just be about my size.'

A breeze rustled the trees of the Park and the coloured drawing seemed to tremble.

'I never can choose between Florimond and Veritain,' Jane murmured. 'They are both so beautiful.'

The fountain gave a laughing ripple and an echo of laughter seemed to come from the book.

'I'll lend it to you!' said the youngest Prince, whipping the dagger from his belt.

'Why not choose us both?' cried the two eldest, stepping forward on to the lawn.

Jane and Michael caught their breath. What had happened? Had the painted forest come to the Park? Or was it that the Rose Garden had gone into the picture? Are we there? Are they here? Which is which? they asked themselves, and could not give an answer.

'Don't you know us, Jane?' asked Florimond, smiling.

'Yes, of course!' she gasped. 'But – how did you get here?'

'Didn't you see?' asked Veritain. 'You smiled at us and we smiled at you. And the picture looked so shiny and bright – you and Michael and the painted roses –'

'So we jumped right into the story!' Amor concluded gaily.

'Out of it, you mean!' cried Michael. 'We're not a story. We're real people. It's you who are the pictures!'

The Princes tossed their curls and laughed.

'Touch me!' said Florimond.

'Take my hand!' urged Veritain.

'Here's my dagger!' cried Amor.

Michael took the golden weapon. It was sharp and solid and warm from Amor's body.

'Who's real now?' Amor demanded. 'Tuck it into your belt,' he said, smiling at Michael's astonished face.

'You see – I was right!' said Florimond, as Jane put one hand on his sleeve and the other in Veritain's outstretched palm. She felt the warmth of both and nodded.

'But –' she protested. 'How can it be? You are in Once Upon a Time. And that is long ago.'

'Oh, no!' said Veritain. 'It's always. Do you remember your great-great-great-great-grandmother?'

'Of course not. I am much too young.'

'We do,' said Florimond with a smile. 'And what about your great-great-great-great-granddaughter? Will you ever see her, do you think?'

Jane shook her head a little wistfully. That charming far-away little girl – how much she would like to know her!

'We shall,' said Veritain confidently.

'But how? You're the children in the story!'

Florimond laughed and shook his head.

'*You* are the children in the story! We've read about you so often, Jane, and looked at the picture and longed to know you. So today – when the book fell open – we simply walked in. We come once into everyone's story – the grandparents and the grandchildren are all the same to us. But most people take no notice.' He sighed. 'Or if they do, they forget very quickly. Only a few remember.'

Jane's hand tightened on his sleeve. She felt *she* would never forget him, not if she lived to be forty.

'Oh, don't waste time explaining,' begged Amor. 'We want to explore the picture!'

'We'll lead the way!' cried Michael eagerly, as he seized Amor by the hand. He hardly cared whether he was a real boy or a boy in a story, so long as the golden dagger lay snugly in his belt.

'We'll follow!' cried Veritain, running behind them.

Florimond gave a piercing whistle and tugged at the rein on his arm.

Immediately, as if from nowhere, the Unicorn appeared at his side. Florimond patted the silky neck and, moving off beside Jane, he glanced about him eagerly.

'Look, brothers – over there is the Lake! Do you see Neleus with his Dolphin? And that must be Number Seventeen. We never could see it clearly before,' he explained to Jane and Michael. 'In the picture it's hidden behind the trees.'

'H'm – a very small house,' said Amor, gazing.

'But it's solid and friendly,' said Veritain kindly.

'And the grounds are very extensive.' Florimond made a sweeping gesture and bent to sniff at a rose.

'Now, now! Wot are you doin'!' The Park Keeper, roused from his Forty Winks, sat up and rubbed his eyes.

'Observe the rules,' he grumbled, stretching. 'No pickin' of flowers allowed.'

'I wasn't picking. I was just smelling. Though, of course,' said Florimond politely, 'I would like to have a rose from Jane's garden. As a souvenir, you know!'

'*Jane's* garden?' The Park Keeper stared. 'This is no garden. It's a Public Park. And it don't belong to Jane. Sooveneer, indeed!' he spluttered. ''Oo do you think you are?'

'Oh, I don't think – I know!' the Prince replied. 'I am Florimond, the King's eldest son. These are my brothers – don't you remember? And our task is to fight the Dragon.'

The Park Keeper's eyes nearly dropped from his head.

'King's eldest –? Dragon? No dragons allowed in the Public Parks. And no horses, neither!' he added, as his eyes fell on the silvery hooves that were lightly pawing the lawn.

A peal of laughter burst from Amor.

Jane and Michael giggled.

'That's not a horse,' Veritain protested. 'Can't you see? He's a Unicorn!'

'Now, now!' The Park Keeper heaved to his feet. 'I ought to know a Norse when I see one and that's a Norse or I'm a – Lumme!'

The milk-white creature raised its head.

'It is! It *is* a Unycorn! 'Orn and all – just like a picture. I never saw such a thing before – at least –' The Park Keeper wrinkled up his brow as though he were trying to remember something. 'No, no,' he murmured, 'I couldn't have! Not even when I was a boy. A Unycorn! I must

make a report. Winkle, where are you?' 'Ere, you boys –'
He turned to the astonished Princes. 'You 'old 'im quiet
till I get back. Don't let him go wotever you do!'

And off he went, leaping over the flower-beds. ''Orn
and all!' they heard him shouting, as he darted among the
laurels.

The Princes, their eyes round with surprise, gazed after
his disappearing figure.

'Your gardener seems very excitable,' said Florimond
to Jane.

She was just about to explain that the Park Keeper was
not their gardener, when a shrill voice interrupted her.

'Wait! Wait! Not so fast! My arms are nearly out of
their sockets. Oh, what shall I do? There goes my scarf!'

Into the Rose Garden plunged Miss Lark, with the two
dogs straining at their leads. Her hat was wobbling dan-
gerously and her hair hung in wisps around her face.

'Oh, goodness! There they go again! Andrew! Willoughby! Do come back!'

But the dogs merely laughed. They tugged the leathers
from her hands and, bounding gaily towards the Princes,
they leapt up at Amor.

'Oh, Jane! Oh, Michael!' Miss Lark panted. 'Do help
me, please, to catch the dogs. I don't like them talking to
strangers. Look at that queer boy kissing Andrew! He
may have a cold and the dogs will catch it. Who *are* these
children? What very odd clothes! And their hair is much
too long!'

'This is Florimond,' said Jane politely.

'This is Veritain,' added Michael.

'And this is Amor!' said Amor, laughing, as he kissed
Willoughby's nose.

'Peculiar names!' exclaimed Miss Lark. 'And yet –' Her
face had a puzzled expression. 'I seem to have heard them
before. Where can it have been? In a pantomime?'

She peered at the Princes and shook her head. 'They're foreigners, without a doubt. And what have they got there – a donkey? Gracious!' She gave a shriek of surprise. 'It can't be! Yes! No! Yes – it is! A Unicorn – how *wonderful*!'

She clasped her hands in ecstasy and trilled away like a lark. 'Horn and all! A Unicorn! But why isn't somebody looking after it?'

'We are looking after him,' said Florimond calmly.

'Nonsense! Ridiculous! Absurd! He should be in charge of responsible people. I shall go myself to the British Museum and find the Chief Professor. Andrew and Willoughby, leave that boy and come along with Mother! Quickly, quickly!' She seized the leads. 'We must go at once for help!'

The two dogs exchanged a wink and dashed away at full speed.

'Oh, not so quickly as that,' cried Miss Lark. 'You will have me head-over-heels. Oh, dear, oh, dear – there goes my bracelet! Never mind!' she called over her shoulder, as Veritain stooped to pick it up. 'Keep it! I've no time to waste!'

And off she stumbled behind the dogs with her hair and necklaces flying.

'Officer!' they heard her calling to the Policeman. 'There's a Unicorn in the Rose Garden. Be sure you don't let him escape!'

'Escape?' said Amor. 'But why should he want to! He'd never be happy away from us.'

He smiled lovingly at Michael as the Unicorn thrust his head between them and tickled their cheeks with his mane.

'A Unicorn!' The Policeman stared. 'Miss Lark's gettin' queerer and queerer!' he muttered, as he watched her fluttering down the path. ''Ere! Look where you're going, Mr Mudge! You can't do that to the Law.'

For a large fat man had bumped into him and was breathlessly hurrying by. The Policeman seized him by the arm.

'A Unicorn, the old girl said!' Mr Mudge panted heavily.

'A Unicorn?' cried the passing strangers. 'We don't believe it! We must write to *The Times*!'

'Of course, I know there's no such thing. Somebody's having a bit of a joke.' Mr Mudge mopped his poppy cheeks. 'But I thought as I'd go and see.'

'Well, you go quietly,' the Policeman advised him. 'And treat the Law with respect.'

He released Mr Mudge's arm and strode on ahead of him.

'Come, let us go deeper into the picture,' Florimond was saying. He took Jane gently by the hand and Veritain came to her other side.

'Hurry up, Michael! Let's try the swings. And then we can paddle in the Lake.' Amor gave a tug to Michael's hand. 'But who are all these people?'

The five children glanced about them. The Park, which had been so quiet before, was now filled with flying figures, all racing towards the Rose Garden and shouting as they came. The Policeman stalked along before them with big, important strides.

As the children turned to leave the garden, his large blue body barred the way.

He gave one glance at the Unicorn and his eyebrows went up to the edge of his helmet.

'Miss Lark was right, after all,' he muttered. Then he eyed the Princes sternly.

'Might I h'ask what you think you're up to – disturbing the peace in a public place? And I'd like to know how you three tinkers got hold of that there animal!'

'They're not tinkers!' protested Michael. He was

116

shocked at the Policeman's words. Couldn't he *see* who they were?

'Gypsies, then. You can tell by their clothes. Too gaudy for respectable people.'

'But don't you remember them?' cried Jane. She was fond of the Policeman and wanted him not to make a mistake.

'Never saw them before in my life.' He took out his notebook and pencil. 'Now, I want a few pertickelers. Honesty's the best policy, lads, so speak up clearly and state the facts. First of all, where do you come from?'

'Nowhere!' giggled Amor.

'Everywhere!' said Veritain.

'East of the Sun and West of the Moon,' Florimond added gravely.

'Now, now! This won't do. I asked a plain question and I want a plain answer. Where do you live? What place on the map?'

'Oh, it's not on the map,' said Florimond. 'But it's easy to find if you really want to. You only have to wish.'

'No fixed address,' the Policeman murmured, writing in his notebook. 'You see! They're gypsies – just like I said. Now then, young man – your father's name!'

'Fidelio,' answered Florimond.

'Mother's name?' The Law gave his pencil a careful lick.

'Esperanza,' Veritain told him. 'With a "Z",' he added helpfully, for the Policeman, it seemed, was not a good speller.

'Aunts?' inquired the Policeman again, laboriously writing.

'Oh, we have hundreds.' Amor grinned. 'Cinderella, Snow White, Badroulbador, the White Cat, Little-Two-Eyes, Baba Yaga – and, of course, the Sleeping Beauty.'

'Sleeping Beauty –' the Policeman murmured.

Then he looked at the words he had written and glanced up angrily.

'You're making a mock of the Law!' he cried. 'The Sleeping Beauty wasn't nobody's aunt. She was somebody in a book. Now, see here! Since you boys refuse to give me h'information in h'accordance with the h'regulations, it is my duty to take that animal in charge.'

He stepped forward resolutely.

The Unicorn gave an angry snort and flung up his hind legs.

''Ands off! 'Ands off!' yelled the Park Keeper, as he flung himself across the roses and pushed the Policeman aside.

'There 'e is, Ben!' he cried in triumph, as the Keeper of the Zoological Gardens, nervously waving his butterfly net, came tiptoeing into the Rose Garden.

''Orn and all – just like I told yer!' The Park Keeper reached for the silver bridle and immediately turned a back somersault.

For the Unicorn had lowered his head and swung his horn against him.

'E-e-eh! Oh! O-o-o-h!' The Keeper of the Zoological Gardens, with a frightened yelp, took refuge behind the Policeman.

'Dear me, is he dangerous? Does he bite? That horn looks very sharp!'

'It's sharp *and* solid, Benjamin!' The Park Keeper ruefully rubbed his stomach.

'He's gentle and good,' Florimond protested. 'But he isn't used to strangers.'

'H'm. Well, you'd better bring him along to the Zoo and settle him down in a cage.'

'A cage! Oh, no,' cried Jane and Michael, angrily stamping their feet.

And the Unicorn, as though in agreement, drummed with his hooves on the lawn.

'But what would he do in a cage?' asked Amor, his eyes wide with interest.

'Do?' echoed the Keeper of the Zoological Gardens. 'He'd do what the other animals do – just stand there to be looked at!'

'Oh, he wouldn't like that,' put in Veritain quickly. 'He's used to being quite free. Besides,' he added, smiling politely, 'he belongs to us, you know!'

'Free!' The Policeman shook his fist. 'Nobody's free to kick at the Law!'

'Whoa there!' cried the Keeper of the Zoological Gardens.

'I *won't* whoa there!' the Policeman shouted. 'I'm only doing what's right!'

'I was talking to *him*,' murmured Mr Winkle. And

he pointed to the Unicorn who was dancing madly on all four feet.

'Now then,' he cooed, 'be a good little Dobbin. And we'll get him some hay and a nice clean house next door to the Hippopotamus!'

The Unicorn gave his tail a twitch and lashed it at Mr Winkle. It was quite clear that he had no intention of living anywhere near a hippopotamus.

'Don't coax 'im, Benjamin, just take 'im!' The Park Keeper gave his friend a push.

'Oh, no! Not yet! Wait just one minute!'

Miss Lark's voice sounded shriller than ever as she hurried back to the scene. In one hand she held up her tattered skirt and with the other she dragged along an elderly gentleman in a newspaper hat. He was carrying a large book and a magnifying-glass and looking very bewildered.

'So fortunate!' Miss Lark panted. 'I found the Professor asleep on a bench. There now, Professor –' She flung out her hand. 'Do you still say you don't believe me?'

'Don't believe what?' the Professor mumbled.

'Tch! Tch! I've told you a dozen times. I've found a Unicorn!'

'Indeed?' The Professor fumbled in his pockets till at length he found his spectacles and fixed them on his nose.

'Er – what was it, dear lady, I had to look at?' He seemed to have quite forgotten what he wanted his spectacles for.

Miss Lark sighed.

'The Unicorn!' she answered patiently.

The Professor blinked and turned his head.

'Well, well! Er – hum! Extraordinary!'

He leaned forward for a closer look and the Unicorn made a thrust with his head and prodded the Professor with the end of his horn.

'You're right!' The Professor toppled backwards. 'It *is* – ah – hum – a Unicorn!'

'Of course it is!' scoffed the Park Keeper. 'We don't need nobody in a paper 'at to tell us that bit o' news.'

The Professor took not the slightest notice. He was turning the pages of his book and waving a magnifying-glass.

'O.P.Q.R.S.T.U. Ah, here it is! Yes. A fabulous beast. Rarely – if ever! – seen by man. Reputed to be worth a city –'

'A city!' exclaimed the Policeman, staring. 'A horse with a bit o' bone on his head!'

'Distinguishing marks –' the Professor gabbled. 'White body, tail of similar hue, and a broad brow from which a horn –'

'Yes, yes, Professor,' Miss Lark broke in. 'We know what he looks like. You needn't tell us. The question is – what shall we do with him?'

'Do?' The Professor looked over the top of his glasses. 'There's only one thing to be done, madam. We must arrange to – ah – have him stuffed!'

'Stuffed?' Miss Lark gave a little gasp. She glanced uneasily at the Unicorn and he gave her a long, reproachful stare.

'Stuffed!' cried Jane in a horrified voice.

'Stuffed!' echoed Michael squeakily. He could hardly bear to think of it.

The Princes shook their golden heads. Their eyes as they gazed at the Professor were grave and full of pity.

'Stuffed? Stuff and nonsense!' said a raucous voice, as Mr Mudge, looking redder than ever, came lumbering into the Rose Garden. 'Nobody's going to stuff an animal that might be of use to Mudge. Where is it?' he demanded loudly.

His bulgy eyes grew bulgier still as they fell on the silver shape.

'Well, I never!' He whistled softly. 'Cleverest dodge I ever saw. Somebody's glued a horn on a horse! My word –

what a sideshow this will make! Who's in charge of the beast?'

'We are,' said Florimond, Veritain and Amor.

Mr Mudge turned and surveyed the Princes.

'Out of the Circus, I see!' He grinned. 'What are you – acrobats?'

The Princes smiled and shook their heads.

'Well, you can come along with the nag. Those velvet jackets are just the thing. Three meals a day and oats for the horse. And I'll bill you as Mudge's Unicorn and his Three Servants. Hey, back up, Neddy – look what you're doing!'

Mr Mudge jumped sideways just in time to escape a nip from the Unicorn's teeth.

'Here, tighten that rein!' he shouted sharply. 'Take care! He's got a nasty temper!'

'Oh, no he hasn't,' said Florimond quickly. 'But he doesn't care to be part of a sideshow.'

'And we're not his servants,' said Veritain.

'It's the other way round!' Amor added.

'Now, I want no sauciness, my lads! Just bring him along and behave yourselves. We've got to get him settled down before the Fair opens.'

The Unicorn tossed his silver mane.

'Begging your pardon, Mr Mudge! But that Unicorn belongs to the Zoo!'

Thump! went the Unicorn's horn on the lawn.

'Nonsense – er – hum!' the Professor exclaimed. 'He must go with me to the British Museum. And stand – ah – hum – on a pedestal for all the world to see.'

'The world can see him in his cage,' said Mr Winkle stubbornly.

'At the Fair, you mean!' Mr Mudge insisted. 'The Only Unicorn in the World! Money back if not satisfied. Roll up! Roll up! Sixpence a look!'

'He belongs to the Princes!' shouted Michael.

But nobody took any notice.

The Park was ringing with many voices. People came running from all directions, all giving different advice.

'Get him a halter! Hobble his legs! Bind him! Hold him! Put him in chains!'

And the Unicorn lashed out with his hooves and swung his horn around like a sword and kept them all at a distance.

'He belongs to the Law!' the Policeman roared, taking out his baton.

'To Mudge's Fair!' cried Mr Mudge. 'Children Half-price! Babies Free!'

'To the Zoo!' squeaked the Keeper of the Zoological Gardens, waving his net in the air.

'What's going on – an accident?' Bert, the Match Man, pushed through the crowd and sauntered into the Rose Garden.

At the sight of his calm and cheerful face, Jane gave a sigh of relief.

'Oh, help us, please!' She ran to him. 'They're trying to take the Unicorn.'

'The *what*?' said the Match Man, very surprised. He glanced at the little group by the fountain and gave a sudden start. A look of joy spread over his face as he sprang across the lawn.

'Gently, boy, gently! Easy does it!' He seized the Unicorn by the mane and held out the apple he was munching. The Unicorn lowered his tossing head, sniffed inquiringly at the outstretched hand and then, with a sigh of satisfaction, he gobbled up the core.

The Match Man gave him a friendly slap. Then he turned to the Princes with a loving look and, falling upon one knee, kissed Florimond's hand.

There was a sudden silence in the Rose Garden. Everybody stared.

'What's the matter with Bert?' the Park Keeper muttered. ''E must 'ave gorn mad!'

For the Match Man had turned to Veritain and Amor and was kissing their hands, too.

'Welcome, my Princes!' he said softly. 'I am happy to see you again!'

'Princes, indeed!' the Policeman exploded. 'A set of rascals, that's what they are. I found them loitering in the Park in wrongful possession of a fabbilous animal. And I'm taking it in charge!'

'What, *that*?' The Match Man glanced at the Unicorn and laughed as he shook his head. 'You wouldn't be able to catch him, Egbert. He isn't your sort of animal. And what's a Unicorn, anyway, compared with the three of them?'

He turned to the Princes with outstretched arms.

'They've forgotten us, Bert,' said Florimond sadly.

'Well, you won't forget *me* in a hurry,' the Policeman put in grimly. 'Move away, Bert, you're obstructing the Law. Now, bring that Unicorn along and follow me, all three!'

'Don't you go, lads,' urged Mr Mudge. 'Just slip along to the Fair Ground and you and horsie will be treated proper.'

'Oh, come with me, boys!' begged Mr Winkle. 'If I let that Unicorn slip through my fingers, the Head Keeper will never forgive me.'

'No!' said Veritain.

'No!' said Amor.

'I am sorry,' said Florimond, shaking his head. 'But we cannot go with any of you.'

'You'll come, if I have to carry you!' The Policeman strode towards the Princes with an angry gleam in his eye.

'Oh, please don't touch them!' Jane cried wildly, flinging herself in his way.

'You leave them alone!' screamed Michael, as he seized the Policeman by the leg.

''Ooligans!' exclaimed Mr Mudge. '*I* never behaved like that!'

'Let me go, Michael!' the Policeman yelled.

'What shocking conduct! How badly brought up!' cried voices in the crowd.

'Professor, Professor, please do something!' Miss Lark's voice rose above the din.

'Such goings on!' murmured Mr Winkle. 'It's worse than the Lion House!'

He turned in terror from the scene and knocked against a moving object that was entering the Rose Garden. A creaking wheel passed over his foot and his net became entangled with a large crimson flower.

'Out of my way!' said Mary Poppins, as she disengaged the net from her hat. 'And I'll thank you to remember,' she added, 'that I'm not a butterfly!'

'I can see that,' said the Keeper of the Zoological Gardens, as he dragged his foot from under the wheel.

Mary Poppins gave him an icy glare as she thrust him calmly out of her way and tripped towards the fountain.

At the sight of her neat and dignified figure there was a moment's silence. The crowd gave her a respectful stare. The Match Man took off his cap.

'Good afternoon, Bert!' she said, with a bow. But the ladylike smile froze on her lips as her glance fell upon the children.

'May I ask what you think you're doing, Jane? And you, too, Michael! Let go that Policeman! Is this a garden or a Cannibal Island?'

'A Cannibal Island!' cried the youngest Prince, laughing with joy as he ran towards her. 'At last! At last, Mary Poppins!' he murmured, as he flung his arms round her waist.

Michael seized the Policeman by the leg

'Mary Poppins! Mary Poppins!' cried the elder brothers as they leapt together over the fountain and seized her kid-gloved hands.

'Whin-n-n-e-e-e-h-o-o-o!' The Unicorn gave a happy neigh and, trotting daintily towards her, he touched his horn to her black-buttoned shoe.

Mary Poppins' eyes darkened.

'Florimond! Veritain! Amor! What are you doing here?'

'Well, the book fell open –'

'At Jane and Michael's story –'

'So we just jumped into the picture –'

The three Princes hung their heads as they all answered together.

'Then you'd better jump out of it – spit-spot! You're very naughty boys!'

Amor gave her a loving smile.

'And you're a naughty girl!' he retorted. 'Going away and leaving us with never a Word of Warning!'

Michael stared. He loosed his hold on the Policeman's leg and ran to Amor.

'Do you know Mary Poppins?' he demanded. 'And did she do that to you, too?' He felt rather jealous of his friend. Would *he* ever be so brave, he wondered, as to call her a naughty girl?

'Of course we know her. And she's always doing it – coming and going without a word. Oh, don't be cross with us, Mary Poppins!' Amor looked up with an impish grin. 'I see you've got a new hat!'

A ghost of a smile crept round her mouth, but she changed it into a sniff.

'Your face is dirty, Amor, as usual!'

And whipping out her lace-edged handkerchief she dabbed it quickly against his tongue, gave his cheek a vigorous rub and tucked the handkerchief into his pocket.

'Hm. That's more like it,' she said tartly. 'Florimond,

put your cap on straight. It was always on one side, I remember. And, Veritain, will you never learn? If I've told you once, I've told you twice, to tie your laces with *double* knots. Just look at your slippers!'

Veritain stooped to his velvet shoes and tied the straggling cords.

'Yes – *you* remember, Mary Poppins!' Florimond straightened the set of his cap. 'But, except for Jane and Michael and Bert, you are the only one. All *they* want is the Unicorn –' He pointed to the watching crowd. 'And they can't even agree about him.'

The Unicorn nodded his silver head and his blue eye blazed with wrath.

'Pooh!' Mary Poppins turned up her nose. 'What else could you expect – from them? It's their misfortune, Florimond. No fault of yours!'

The Policeman blushed as red as a beetroot beneath her

scornful gaze.

'I remember my duty!' he said doggedly.

'I remember the public's entertainment!' Mr Mudge bristled.

'I remember the Head Keeper!' whispered the Keeper of the Zoological Gardens.

'Wait! I remember something else!' The Park Keeper clapped his hand to his brow.

''Arf a minute – it's comin' back. I can see me old mother readin' aloud. A silver book. And the cat by the fire. And them –' He flung out a hand to the Princes.

'And them and me goin' 'and in 'and. There was flower and fruit on the same branch and a Unycorn trottin' through the forest. Oh, what 'as 'appened?' he cried aloud. 'Me 'eart is beatin' the way it used to! I feel like I felt when I was a boy. No litter, no bye-laws, no Lord Mayor, and sausages for supper. Oh, now I remember you, Mister – er – Prince –'

The Park Keeper turned to Florimond. His sombre face had quite changed. It was gleaming with happiness.

'A sooveneer!' he shouted gaily. 'Something for you to remember me by!'

And recklessly he dashed at the flower-beds and snapped off three of the largest roses.

'I shall get into trouble, but what do I care! I'm doin' it for you!' With a shy and humble gesture, he thrust the flowers at Florimond.

Grave and glad were Florimond's eyes as he touched the Park Keeper's cheek.

'Thank you.' He smiled. 'I shall keep them always.'

'Aw!' The Park Keeper gave an embarrassed laugh. 'You can't do that. They'll fade, you know!'

'Oh, no, they won't!' cried Miss Lark suddenly. 'In their country, dear Park Keeper, the roses bloom for ever.'

She turned to the Princes eagerly, with her hands against her heart.

'Oh, how could I have forgotten?' she murmured. 'It was yesterday – or the day before! I was wearing a pinafore tied at the back –'

'And button-boots,' put in Veritain.

'And yellow curls with a blue ribbon,' said Amor helpfully. 'She does remember!' he cried to his brothers, smiling at Miss Lark.

'And you were everywhere!' she whispered. 'Playing beside me in the sunlight, swinging with me on the garden gate. The birds in the trees were you disguised. I stepped over every ant and beetle for fear it might be one of my Princes. I meant to marry a King – I remember – or at least a Caliph's younger son. And you three were to be always near me. And then – oh, what happened? How did I lose you? Was it really only yesterday? Where are my curls, my yellow curls? Why am I all alone in the world, except for two little dogs?'

Andrew and Willoughby glanced up indignantly. 'Except, indeed!' they seemed to say.

'Yes, yes, I'm getting old,' said Miss Lark, as she peered through her wisps of hair. 'I'll forget you again, my darling Princes! But, oh, do not forget me! What shall I give you to remember me by? I have lost' – she scrabbled in her pockets – 'so many of my possessions!'

'We will never forget you,' said Veritain gently. 'And you've given us something already.'

He drew his velvet sleeve aside and showed her the glitter at his wrist.

'My bracelet! But it's only glass!'

'No!' cried Veritain. 'Rubies! Sapphires!'

He raised his hand above his head and the bracelet shone so bright in the sunset that it dazzled every eye.

'Golly!' the Policeman muttered. 'He's stolen the Crown Jewels!'

'Oh!' breathed Miss Lark, as she clasped her hands and gazed at the shining stones.

'I understand,' she murmured softly. 'Professor, Professor, do you see?'

But the Professor put his hand to his eyes and turned his head away.

'I have seen too much,' he said sadly. 'I have seen how foolish I am! Books!' he cried, tossing the volume from him. 'Magnifying-glasses!' He flung the glass among the roses. 'Alas, alas! I have wasted my time. Florimond, Veritain, Amor – I recognize you now!' He turned his tearful face to the Princes.

'Oh, Beauty, Truth and Love,' he whispered. 'To think that I knew you when I was a lad! To think that I could forget! All day long you ran at my side. And your voices called to me in the dusk – Follow! Follow! Follow! I see it now – I've been looking for wisdom. But wisdom was there and I turned my back. I've been running away from it ever since, trying to find it in books. So far away' – the Professor hid his face in his arm – 'that when I met a Unicorn, I imagined I could have him stuffed! Oh, how can I make up for that? I have no rose, no jewels, nothing.'

He glanced about him doubtfully and put his hand to his forehead. And as he did so his face cleared. A happy thought had struck him.

'Take this, my child!' he said to Amor, as he plucked the newspaper hat from his brow. 'Your way is long and the night will be chilly and you've nothing on your head!'

'Thank you, Professor!' Amor smiled and set the hat at a jaunty angle over his crown of curls. 'I hope you will not be cold without it.'

'Cold?' the Professor murmured vaguely, as his gaze slipped past the Princes to the snow-white creature on the lawn. He put out an aged, trembling hand and the Unicorn rose from the dewy grass and calmly came to his side.

'Forgive me!' the Professor whispered. 'It was not I that would have stuffed you. A madman wearing my skin – not I! No, no! I'll never be cold again. I have stroked a Unicorn!'

His fingers touched the milky neck. The Unicorn stood mild and still. His blue eyes did not flicker.

'That's right, Professor!' said the Policeman cheerfully. 'No good trying to stuff a h'animal that by rights belongs to the Law!'

'He belongs to the Law,' the Professor murmured. 'But not the Law you know –'

'The Fair!' insisted Mr Mudge, elbowing past the Policeman.

'Yes! All is Fair where he comes from.' The Professor stroked the Unicorn's nose.

'He'll be among the stars of the Zoo,' the Zoo Keeper promised breathlessly.

'He'll be among the stars,' said the Professor, touching the tip of the Unicorn's horn, 'but far, far from the Zoo.'

'Exactly, Professor! You're a sensible chap! Now, I've no more time for h'argument. The boys and the beast are under arrest and I'm taking them off to the Police Station!'

The Policeman put out a determined hand and seized the Unicorn's bridle.

'Quick, Florimond!' warned Mary Poppins.

And Florimond, with a single bound, leapt on the Unicorn's back.

Up went Veritain behind him.

'Good-bye, Michael,' whispered Amor, hugging him round the waist. Then with a graceful, running leap he landed behind his brothers.

'Oh, do not leave me!' cried Miss Lark. 'I may forget again!'

'I won't forget!' said Michael stoutly, waving his hand to Amor.

'Nor I! Oh, never!' echoed Jane, with a long look at

Florimond and Veritain. She felt that their faces were in her heart for ever.

'If you remember, we'll come again!' Florimond promised, smiling. 'Are you ready, my brothers? We must go!'

'Ready!' the younger Princes cried.

Then one by one they leant sideways and kissed Mary Poppins.

'We'll be waiting for you,' said Florimond.

'Do not be long!' urged Veritain.

'Come back to us,' said Amor, laughing, 'with a tulip in your hat!'

She tried to look stern, but she simply couldn't. Her firm lips trembled into a smile as she gazed at their shining faces.

'Get along with you – and behave yourselves!' she said with surprising softness.

Then she raised her parrot-headed umbrella and touched the Unicorn's flank.

At once he lifted his silver head and pointed his horn at the sky.

'Remember!' cried Florimond, waving his roses.

Veritain held his hand aloft and set the bracelet sparkling.

Amor flourished the handkerchief.

'Remember! Remember!' they cried together, as the Unicorn bounded into the air.

The Park seemed to tremble in the fading light as his hooves flashed over the fountain. A streak of colour shone above the spray, a shimmer of velvet and gold. A single moment of moving brightness and after that – nothing. Princes and Unicorn were gone. Only a far, faint echo – 'Remember!' came back to the silent watchers. And the pages of the book on the lawn stirred in the evening breeze.

'After them!' the Policeman shouted. 'Robbers! Desperadoes!'

He blew his whistle vigorously and dashed across the Rose Garden.

'A trick! A trick!' yelled Mr Mudge. 'The Invisible Horse and his Three Riders! Why, it's better than Sawing a Lady in Half! Come back, my lads, and I'll buy your secret! Was it this way? That way? Where did they go?'

And off he went, dodging among the trees, in his search for the lost Princes.

'Oh, dear,' moaned the Keeper of the Zoological Gardens. 'Here today and gone tomorrow! Just like the butterflies!'

He gave Mary Poppins a nervous look and hurried away to the Zoo.

For a moment the only sound in the garden was the

music of the fountain. Then Miss Lark sighed and broke the silence.

'Why, goodness me – how late it is! Now, I wonder where I left my gloves! And what did I do with my scarf? I seem to have lost my spectacles. Gracious, yes – and my bracelet, too!'

Her eyes widened and she yawned a little as though she were coming out of a dream.

'You gave it to Veritain!' Jane reminded her.

'Veritain? Veritain? Who can that be? It sounds like something out of a story. I expect you are dreaming, Jane, as usual! Andrew and Willoughby – come along! Oh, Chief Professor! How nice to see you! But what are you doing here?'

The Professor gave her a puzzled glance and he, too, yawned a little.

'I – I'm not quite sure,' he answered vaguely.

'And without a hat – you must be cold! Come home with me, Professor, do! And we'll all have muffins for tea.'

'Muffins? Er – hum. I used to like muffins when I was a lad, but I haven't had one since. And I had a hat this afternoon. Now, what have I done with it?'

'Amor is wearing it!' cried Michael.

'Amor? Is that a friend of yours? He's welcome! It was only paper. But I'm not a bit cold, Miss Lark – er – hum! I have never felt so warm in my life.'

The Professor smiled a contented smile.

'And I,' said Miss Lark with a trill of laughter, 'have never felt so happy. I can't think why – but there it is. Come, dearest dogs! This way, Professor!'

And, taking the Professor by the hand, she led him out of the Rose Garden.

Jane and Michael stared after them.

'What is your other – er – hum! – name?' they heard him vaguely asking.

'Lucinda Emily,' she replied as she drew him towards the Gate.

'Eee – ow – oo! I was 'arf asleep!' The Park Keeper yawned and stretched his arms and glanced around the garden.

''Ere! Wot's all this?' he demanded loudly. 'Someone's been pickin' the flowers!'

'You did it yourself,' said Jane, laughing.

'Don't you remember?' Michael reminded him. 'You gave them to Florimond.'

'What? Me pick a rose? I wouldn't dare! And yet –' The Park Keeper frowned in perplexity. 'It's funny. I'm feeling quite brave tonight. If the Lord Mayor himself were to come along, I wouldn't so much as tremble. And why shouldn't Florrie Wat's-a-name 'ave them, instead of them dyin' on the bush? Well, I must be gettin' 'ome to me mother. Tch! Tch! Tch! Remember the bye-laws!' The Park Keeper pounced on two dark objects.

'All litter to be placed in the baskets!' he cried, as he bore away the Professor's book and magnifying-glass and dumped them into a litter-basket.

Jane sighed. 'They've forgotten already, all of them. Miss Lark, the Professor, and now the Park Keeper.'

'Yes,' agreed Michael, shaking his head.

'And what have *you* forgotten, pray?' Mary Poppins' eyes were bright in the sunset and she seemed to come back to the Rose Garden from very far away.

'Oh, nothing, Mary Poppins, nothing!' With the happy assurance they ran to her side. As if they could ever forget the Princes and the strange and wonderful visit!

'Then what is that book doing there?' She pointed her black-gloved finger at *The Silver Fairy Book*.

'Oh, that!' Michael darted to get it.

'Wait for me, Mary Poppins!' he cried, pushing his way

through the watching crowd that was still staring up at the sky.

The Match Man took the perambulator and sent it creaking out of the garden. Mary Poppins stood still in the entrance with her parrot umbrella under her arm and her handbag hanging from her wrist.

'I remember *everything*,' said Michael, as he hurried back to her side. 'And so does Jane – don't you – Jane? And you do, too, Mary Poppins!' The three of us, he thought to himself, we all remember together.

Mary Poppins quickened her steps and they caught up with the perambulator.

'I remember that I want my tea, if that's what you mean!' she said.

'I wonder if Amor drinks tea!' mused Michael, running beside her.

'Tea!' cried the Match Man, thirstily. 'Hot and strong, that's how I like it. And at least three lumps of sugar!'

'Do you think they're nearly home, Mary Poppins? How long is it from here to there?' Michael was thinking about the Princes. He could not get them out of his head.

'*I'm* nearly home, that's all I know,' she replied conceitedly.

'They'll come again, they said they would!' He skipped with joy at the thought. Then he remembered something else and stood stock-still with dismay.

'But you won't go back to them, Mary Poppins?' He seized her arm and shook it. 'We need you more than the Princes do. They've got the Unicorn – that's enough. Oh, p-p-please, Mary P-pop-pins –' He was now so anxious he could hardly speak. 'P-p-promise me you won't go back with a t-t-tulip in your hat!'

She stared at him in angry astonishment.

'Princes with tulips in their hats? Me on the back of a Unicorn? If you're so good at remembering, I'll thank you to remember *me*! Am I the kind of person that would gallop around on a –'

'No, no! You're mixing it all up. You don't understand, Mary Poppins!'

'I understand that you're behaving like a Hottentot. Me on a Unicorn, indeed! Let me go, Michael, if you please. I hope I can walk without assistance. And you can do the same!'

'Oh! Oh! She's forgotten already!' he wailed, turning to Jane for comfort.

'But the Match Man remembers, don't you, Bert?' Impulsively Jane ran to him and looked for his reassuring smile.

The Match Man took no notice. He was pushing the perambulator on a zigzag course and gazing at Mary Poppins. You would have thought she was the only person in the world, the way he looked at her.

'You see! He's forgotten, too,' said Michael. 'But it must have happened, mustn't it, Jane? After all, I've got the dagger!'

He felt for the dagger in his belt, but his hand closed on nothing.

'It's gone!' he stared at her mournfully. 'He must have taken it when he hugged me good-bye. Or else it wasn't true at all. Do you think we only dreamed it?'

'Perhaps,' she answered uncertainly, glancing from the empty belt to the calm and unexcited faces of the Match Man and Mary Poppins. 'But, oh' – she thought of Florimond's smiling eyes – 'I was so sure they were real!'

They took each other's hands for comfort and leaning their heads on each other's shoulders they walked along together, thinking of the three bright figures and the gentle fairy steed.

Dusk fell about them as they went. The trees like shadows bent above them. And as they came to the big gate they stepped into a pool of light from the newly lit lamp in the Lane.

'Let's look at them once again,' said Jane. Sad it would be, but also sweet, to see their pictured faces. She took the book from Michael's hand and opened it at the well-known page.

'Yes! The dagger's in his belt,' she murmured. 'Just as it always was.' Then her eyes roved over the rest of the picture and she gave a quick, glad cry.

'Oh, Michael, look! It was not a dream. I knew, I *knew* it was true!'

'Where? Where? Show me quickly!' He followed her pointing finger.

'Oh!' he cried, drawing in his breath. And 'Oh!' he said. And again 'Oh!' There was nothing else to say.

For the picture was not as it had been. The fruits and

flowers still shone on the tree and there on the grass the Princes stood with the Unicorn beside them.

But now in the crook of Florimond's arm there lay a bunch of roses; a little circlet of coloured stones gleamed on Veritain's wrist; Amor was wearing a paper hat perched on the back of his head and from the pocket of his jerkin there peeped a lace-edged handkerchief.

Jane and Michael smiled down on the page. And the three Princes smiled up from the book and their eyes seemed to twinkle in the lamplight.

'They remember us!' declared Jane in triumph.

'And we remember them!' crowed Michael. 'Even if Mary Poppins doesn't.'

'Oh, indeed?' her voice inquired behind them.

They glanced up quickly and there she stood, a pink-cheeked Dutch Doll figure, as neat as a new pin.

'And what have I forgotten, pray?'

She smiled as she spoke, but not at them. Her eyes were fixed on the three Princes. She nodded complacently at the picture and then at the Match Man who nodded back.

And suddenly Michael understood. He knew that she remembered. How could he and Jane have dared to imagine that she would ever forget!

He turned and hid his face in her skirt.

'You've forgotten nothing, Mary Poppins. It was just my little mistake.'

'Little!' She gave an outraged sniff.

'But tell me, Mary Poppins,' begged Jane, as she looked from the coloured picture-book to the confident face above her. 'Which are the children in the story – the Princes, or Jane and Michael?'

Mary Poppins was silent for a moment. She glanced at the children on the printed page and back to the living children before her. Her eyes were as blue as the Unicorn's, as she took Jane's hand in hers.

They waited breathlessly for her answer.

It seemed to tremble on her lips. The words were on the tip of her tongue. And then – she changed her mind. Perhaps she remembered that Mary Poppins never told anyone anything.

She smiled a tantalizing smile.

'I wonder!' she said.

CHAPTER FIVE

The Park in the Park

'Another sandwich, please!' said Michael sprawling across Mary Poppins' legs as he reached for the picnic basket.

It was Ellen's Day Out and Mrs Brill had gone to see her cousin's niece's new baby. So the children were having tea in the Park, away by the Wild Corner.

This was the only place in the Park that was never mown or weeded. Clover, daisies, buttercups, bluebells, grew as high as the children's waists. Nettles and dandelions flaunted their blossoms, for they knew very well that the Park Keeper would never have time to root them out. None of them observed the rules. They scattered their seeds across the lawns, jostled each other for the best places, and crowded together so closely that their stems were always in shadowy darkness.

Mary Poppins, in a sprigged cotton dress, sat bolt upright in a clump of bluebells.

She was thinking, as she darned the socks, that pretty though the Wild Corner was, she knew of something prettier. If it came to a choice between, say, a bunch of clover and herself, it would not be the clover she would choose.

The four children were scattered about her.

Annabel bounced in the perambulator.

And not far off, among the nettles, the Park Keeper was making a daisy-chain.

Birds were piping on every bough, and the Ice Cream Man sang cheerfully as he trundled his barrow along.

The notice on the front said:

THE DAY IS HOT
BUT ICE-CREAM'S NOT

'I wonder if he's coming here,' Jane murmured to herself.

She was lying face downwards in the grass, making little Plasticine figures.

'Where *have* those sandwiches gone?' cried Michael, scrabbling in the basket.

'Be so kind, Michael, as to get off my legs. I am not a Turkey carpet! The sandwiches have all been eaten. You had the last yourself.'

Mary Poppins heaved him on to the grass and took up her darning needle. Beside her, a mug of warm tea, sprinkled with grass seed and nettle flowers, sent up a delicious fragrance.

'But, Mary Poppins, I've only had six!'

'That's three too many,' she retorted. 'You've eaten your share and Barbara's.'

'Takin' the food from 'is sister's mouth – what next?' said the Park Keeper.

He sniffed the air and licked his lips, just like a thirsty dog.

'Nothin' to beat a 'ot cup o' tea!' he remarked to Mary Poppins.

With dignified calm she took up the mug. 'Nothing,' she answered, sipping.

'Exactly what a person needs at the 'eight of the h'afternoon!' He gave the teapot a wistful glance.

'Exactly,' she agreed serenely, as she poured herself another cup.

The Park Keeper sighed and plucked a daisy. The pot, he knew, was now empty.

'Well – another sponge cake, then, Mary Poppins!'

'The cakes are finished, too, Michael. What are you, pray – a boy or a crocodile?'

He would have liked to say he was a crocodile, but a glance at her face was enough to forbid it.

'John!' he coaxed, with a crocodile smile. 'Would you like me to eat your crusts?'

'No!' said John, as he gobbled them up.

'Shall I help you with your biscuit, Barbara?'

'No!' she protested through the crumbs.

Michael shook his head in reproach and turned to Annabel.

There she sat, like a queen in her carriage, clutching her little mug. The perambulator groaned loudly as she bounced up and down. It was looking more battered than ever today. For Robertson Ay, after doing nothing all the morning, had leaned against it to take a rest and broken the wooden handle.

'Oh, dear! Oh, dear!' Mrs Banks had cried. 'Why couldn't he lean on something stronger? Mary Poppins, what shall we do? We can't afford a new one!'

'I'll take it to my cousin, ma'am. He'll make it as good as new.'

'Well – if you think he really can –' Mrs Banks cast a doubtful eye on the bar of splintered wood.

Mary Poppins drew herself up.

'A member of *my* family, ma'am –' Her voice seemed to come from the North Pole.

'Oh, yes! Indeed! Quite so! Exactly!' Mrs Banks nervously backed away.

'But why,' she silently asked herself, 'is her family so superior? She is far too vain and self-satisfied. I shall tell her so some day.'

But, looking at that stern face and listening to those reproving sniffs, she knew she would never dare.

Michael rolled over among the daisies, hungrily chewing a blade of grass.

'When are you going to take the perambulator to your cousin, Mary Poppins?'

'Everything comes to him who waits. All in my own good time!'

'Oh! Well, Annabel isn't taking her milk. Would you like me to drink it for her?'

But at that moment Annabel lifted her mug and drained the last drop.

'Mary Poppins!' he wailed. 'I'll starve to death – just like Robinson Crusoe.'

'He didn't starve to death,' said Jane. She was busily clearing a space in the weeds.

'Well, the Swiss Family Robinson, then,' said Michael.

'The Swiss Family always had plenty to eat. But I'm not hungry, Michael. You can have my cake if you like.'

'Dear, kind, sensible Jane!' he thought, as he took the cake.

'What are you making?' he inquired, flinging himself on the grass beside her.

'A Park for Poor People,' she replied. 'Everyone is happy there. And nobody ever quarrels.'

She tossed aside a handful of leaves and he saw, amid the wildweed, a tidy square of green. It was threaded with little pebbled paths as wide as a finger-nail. And beside them were tiny flower-beds made of petals massed together. A summer-house of nettle twigs nestled on the lawn; flowers were stuck in the earth for trees; and in their shade stood twig benches, very neat and inviting.

On one of these sat a Plasticine man, no more than an inch high. His face was round, his body was round and so were his arms and legs. The only pointed thing about him was his little turned-up nose. He was reading a Plasticine newspaper and a Plasticine tool-bag lay at his feet.

'Who's that?' asked Michael. 'He reminds me of someone. But I can't think who it is!'

Jane thought for a moment.

'His name is Mr Mo,' she decided. 'He is resting after his morning labours. He had a wife sitting next to him, but her hat went wrong, so I crumbled her up. I'll try again with the last of the Plasticine –' She glanced at the shapeless, coloured lump that lay behind the summer-house.

'And that?' He pointed to a feminine figure that stood by one of the flower-beds.

'That's Mrs Hickory,' said Jane. 'She's going to have a house, too. And after that I shall build a Fun Fair.'

He gazed at the plump little Plasticine woman and admired the way her hair curled and the two large dimples in her cheeks.

'Do she and Mr Mo know each other?'

'Oh, yes. They meet on the way to the Lake.'

And she showed him a little pebbly hollow where, when Mary Poppins' head was turned, she had poured her mug of milk. At the end of the lake a Plasticine statue reminded Michael of Neleus.

'Or down by the swing –' She pointed to two upright sticks from which an even smaller stick hung on a strand of darning wool.

Michael touched the swing with his finger-tip and it swayed backwards and forwards.

'And what's that under the buttercup?'

A scrap of cardboard from the lid of the cake-box had been bent to form a table. Around it stood several cardboard stools and upon it was spread a meal so tempting that a king might have envied it.

In the centre stood a two-tiered cake and around it were bowls piled high with fruit – peaches, cherries, bananas, oranges. One end of the table bore an apple-pie and the other a ham in a pink ham-frill. There were sausages, and currant buns, and a pat of butter on a little green platter. Each place was set with a plate and a mug and a bottle of ginger wine.

The buttercup-tree spread over the feast. Jane had set two Plasticine doves in its branches and a bumble-bee buzzed among its flowers.

'Go away, greedy fly!' cried Michael, as a small black shape settled on the ham. 'Oh, dear! How hungry it makes me feel!'

Jane gazed with pride at her handiwork. 'Don't drop your crumbs on the lawn, Michael. They make it look untidy.'

'I don't see any litter-baskets. All I can see is an ant in the grass.' He swept his eyes round the tiny Park, so neat amid the wildweed.

'There is never any litter,' said Jane. 'Mr Mo lights the

fire with his paper. And he saves his orange peel for
Christmas puddings. Oh, Michael, don't bend down so
close, you're keeping the sun away!'

His shadow lay over the Park like a cloud.

'Sorry!' he said, as he bent sideways. And the sunlight
glinted down again as Jane lifted Mr Mo and his tool-bag
and set them beside the table.

'Is it his dinner-time?' asked Michael.

'Well – no!' said a little scratchy voice. 'As a matter of
fact, it's breakfast!'

'How clever Jane is!' thought Michael admiringly. 'She
can not only make a little old man, she can talk like one as
well.'

But her eyes, as he met them, were full of questions.

'Did *you* speak, Michael, in that squeaky way?'

'Of course he didn't,' said the voice again.

And, turning, they saw that Mr Mo was waving his hat
in greeting. His rosy face was wreathed in smiles and his
turned-up nose had a cheerful look.

'It isn't what you call the meal. It's how it tastes that
matters. Help yourself!' he cried to Michael. 'A growing
lad is always hungry. Take a piece of pie!'

'I'm having a beautiful dream,' thought Michael, hurriedly helping himself.

'Don't eat it, Michael. It's Plasticine!'

'It's not! It's apple!' he cried, with his mouth full.

'But I know! I made it myself!' Jane turned to Mr Mo.

'You did?' Mr Mo seemed very surprised. 'I suppose
you mean you *helped* to make it. Well, I'm very glad you
did, my girl. Too many cooks make delicious broth!'

'They spoil it, you mean,' corrected Jane.

'Oh, no, no! Not in my opinion. One puts one thing,
one another – oatmeal, cucumber, pepper, tripe. The mer-
rier the more, you know!'

'The more of what?' asked Michael, staring.

'Everything!' Mr Mo replied. 'There's more of everything when one's merry. Take a peach!' He turned to
Jane. 'It matches your complexion.'

From sheer politeness – for she could not disappoint
that smiling face – Jane took the fruit and tasted. Refresh-
ing juice ran over her chin, the peach-stone grated against
her teeth.

'Delicious!' she cried in astonishment.

'Of course it is!' crowed Mr Mo. 'As my dear wife
always used to say – "You can't go by the look of a thing,
it's what's inside that matters."'

'What happened to her?' asked Michael politely, as he
helped himself to an orange. He had quite forgotten, in the
joy of finding more to eat, that Jane had crumbled her up.

'I lost her,' murmured Mr Mo. He gave his head a
sorrowful shake as he popped the orange peel into his
pocket.

Jane felt herself blushing.

'Well – her hat wouldn't sit on straight,' she faltered. But now it seemed to her that this was hardly a good enough reason for getting rid of the hat's owner.

'I know, I know! She was always rather an awkward shape. Nothing seemed to fit her. If it wasn't her hat it was her boots. Even so – I was fond of her.' Mr Mo heaved a heavy sigh. 'However,' he went on gloomily, 'I've found another one!'

'Another wife?' cried Jane in surprise. She knew she had not made two Mrs Mo's. 'But you haven't had time for that!'

'No time? Why, I've all the time in the world. Look at those dandelions!' He waved his chubby hand round the Park. 'And I had to have someone to care for the children. Can't do everything myself. So – I troubled trouble before it troubled me and got myself married just now. This feast here is our wedding-breakfast. But, alas –' He glanced around him nervously. 'Every silver lining has a cloud. I'm afraid I made a bad choice.'

'Coo-roo! Coo-roo!
We told you so!'

cried the Plasticine doves from their branch.

'Children?' said Jane, with a puzzled frown. She was sure she had made no children.

'Three fine boys,' Mr Mo said proudly. 'Surely you two have heard of them! Hi!' he shouted, cupping his hands. 'Eenie, Meenie, Mynie – where are you?'

Jane and Michael stared at each other and then at Mr Mo.

'Oh, of course we've heard of them,' agreed Michael.

'"Eenie, Meenie, Mynie, Mo,
Catch an Indian by the –"

But I thought they were only words in a game.'

Mr Mo smiled a teasing smile.

'Take my advice, my dear young friend, and don't do too much thinking. Bad for the appetite. Bad for the brain. The more you think, the less you know, as my dear – er – first wife used to say. But I can't spend all day chattering, much as I enjoy it!' He plucked a dandelion ball and blew the seeds on the air.

'Goodness, yes, it's four o'clock. And I've got a job to do.'

He took from his tool-bag a piece of wood and began to polish it with his apron.

'What kind of work do you do?' asked Michael.

'Can't you read?' cried the chubby man, waving towards the summer-house.

They turned to Jane's little shelter of twigs and saw to their surprise that it had grown larger. The sticks were solid logs of wood and instead of the airy space between them there were now white walls and curtained windows. Above them rose a new thatched roof, and a sturdy chimney puffed forth smoke. The entrance was closed by a red front door bearing a white placard.

S. MO   (it said)
BUILDER
AND
CARPENTER

'But I didn't build the house like that! Who altered it?' Jane demanded.

'I did, of course.' Mr Mo grinned. 'Couldn't live in it as it was – far too damp and draughty. What did you say – *you* built my house?' He chuckled at the mere idea. 'A little wisp of a lass like you, not as high as my elbow!'

This was really too much for Jane.

'It's you who are little,' she protested. 'I made you of

straw and Plasticine! You're not as big as my thumb!'

'Ha, ha! That's a good one. Made me of hay while the sun shone – is that what you're telling me? Straw, indeed!' laughed Mr Mo. 'You're just like my children – always dreaming. And wonderful dreams they are!'

He gave her head a little pat. And as he did so she realized that she was not, indeed, as high as his elbow. Beneath the branch of yellow blossoms Mr Mo towered above her. The lawns that she herself had plucked now stretched to a distant woodland. And beyond that nothing could she see. The big Park had entirely disappeared, as the world outside disappears when we cross the threshold of home.

She looked up. The bumble-bee seemed like a moving cloud. The shimmering fly that darted past was about the size of a starling and the ant that gave her a bright black stare was nearly as high as her ankle.

What had happened? Had Mr Mo grown taller, or was it that she herself had dwindled? It was Michael who answered the question.

'Jane! Jane!' he cried. 'We're in your Park. I thought it was just a tiny patch, but now it's as big as the world!'

'Well, I wouldn't say that,' Mr Mo observed. 'It only stretches as far as the forest, but it's big enough for us.'

Michael turned, at his words, towards the woodland. It was dense and wild and mysterious, and some of the trees had giant blooms.

'Daisies the size of umbrellas!' he gasped. 'And bluebells large enough to bathe in!'

'Yes, it's a wonderful wood,' Mr Mo agreed, eyeing the forest with a carpenter's eye. 'My – er – second wife wants me to cut it down and sell it to make my fortune. But this is a Park for Poor People. What would I do with a fortune? My own idea – but that was before the wedding, of course – was to build a little Fun Fair –'

'I thought of that, too,' Jane broke in, smiling.

'Well, happy minds think alike, you know! What do you say to a merry-go-round? A coconut-shy, and some swinging-boats? And free to all, friends and strangers alike? Hurrah, I knew you'd agree with me!' He clapped his hands excitedly. But suddenly the eager look died away from his face.

'Oh, it's no good planning,' he went on sadly. '*She* doesn't approve of Fun Fairs – too frivolous and no money in them. What a terrible mistake I've made – married in haste to repent at leisure! But it's no good crying over spilt milk!'

Mr Mo's eyes brimmed up with tears, and Jane was just about to offer him her handkerchief when a clatter of feet sounded on the lawn and his face suddenly brightened.

'Papa!' cried a trio of squeaky voices. And three little figures sprang over the path and flung themselves into his arms. They were all alike, as peas in a pod; and the image of their father.

'Papa, we caught an Indian! We caught him by the toe, Papa! But he hollered, Papa, so we let him go!'

'Quite right, my lads!' smiled Mr Mo. 'He'll be happier in the forest.'

'Indians?' Michael's eyes widened. 'Among those daisy-trees?'

'He was looking for a squaw, Papa, to take care of his wigwam.'

'Well, I hope he finds one,' said Mr Mo. 'Oh, yes, of course there are Indians! And goodness only knows what else. Quite like a jungle, you might say. We never go very far in, you know. Much too dangerous. But – let me introduce my sons. This is Eenie, this is Meenie, and this is Mynie!'

Three pairs of blue eyes twinkled, three pointed noses

turned up to the sky, and three round faces grinned.

'And these –' said Mr Mo, turning. Then he chuckled and flung up his hands. 'Well! Here we are, old friends already, and I don't even know your names!'

They told him, shaking hands with his children.

'Banks? Not the Banks of Cherry Tree Lane? Why, I'm doing a job for you!' Mr Mo rummaged in his tool-bag.

'What kind of job?' demanded Michael.

'It's a new – ah, there you are, Mrs Hickory!'

Mr Mo turned and waved a greeting as a dumpy little feminine figure came hurrying towards them. Two dimples twinkled in her cheeks, two rosy babies bounced in her arms, and she carried in her looped-up apron a large, bulky object.

'But she had no children!' said Jane to herself, as she stared at the two fat babies.

'We've brought you a present, Mr Mo!' Mrs Hickory blushed and opened her apron. 'I found this lovely loaf on the lawn – somebody dropped it, I expect. My twins – this is Dickory, this is Dock,' she explained to the astonished children – 'are far too young to eat fresh bread. So here it is for the breakfast!'

'That's not a loaf, it's a sponge-cake crumb. I dropped it myself,' said Michael. But he could not help feeling that the crumb was a good deal larger than he remembered it.

'Tee-hee!'

Mrs Hickory giggled shyly and her dimples went in and out. You could see she thought he was joking and that she liked being joked with.

'A neighbourly thought!' said Mr Mo. 'Let's cut it in two and have half each. Half a loaf's better than no bread! And, in return, Mrs Hickory, may I give you a speck of butter?'

'Indeed you may NOT!' said a furious voice. And the door of Mr Mo's house burst open.

Jane and Michael fell back a pace. For there stood the largest and ugliest woman they had ever seen in their lives. She seemed to be made of a series of knobs, rather like a potato. A knob of a nose, a knob of hair, knobbly hands, knobbly feet, and her mouth had only two teeth.

She was more like a lump of clay than a human being and Jane was reminded of the scrap of Plasticine that had lain behind the summer-house. A dingy pinafore covered her body and in one of her large, knobbly hands she held a rolling-pin.

'May I ask what you think you're doing, Samuel? Giving away *my* butter?'

She stepped forward angrily and flourished the rolling-pin.

'I – I thought we could spare it, my – er – dear!' Mr Mo quailed beneath her gaze.

'Not unless she pays for it! Spare, spare and your back will go bare!'

'Oh, no, my dear, you've got it wrong! Spare, spare and you'll know no care. Poor people must share and share alike – that's what makes them happy!'

'Nobody's going to share anything that belongs to Matilda Mo! Or spare either, if it comes to that. Last week you spared a footstool for your cousin, Mrs Corry! And what have you got to show for it?'

'A lucky threepenny-piece from her coat!'

'Tush! And you mended a table for the Turvys –'

'Well, Topsy gave me a charming smile!' Mr Mo beamed at the sweet recollection.

157

'Smiles won't fill a sack with gold! And the week before that it was Albert Wigg who wanted his ceiling raised.'

'Well, he needed more room to bounce about in. And it gave me so much pleasure, Matilda!'

'Pleasure? Where's the profit in that? In future you can get your pleasure by giving things to *me*. And you, too!' added Mrs Mo, shaking her fist at the boys.

'Alas, alas!' muttered Mr Mo. 'No rose without a thorn! No joy without annoy!'

'Eenie!' Mrs Mo shouted. 'Get me a wedding-wreath this instant! Look at me – a blushing bride – and nothing on my head.'

'Oh, no!' breathed Jane. 'You'll spoil my garden!'

But Eenie, with a look of alarm, had already darted to the flower-beds and plucked a crown of flowers.

'Not good enough, but better than nothing!' Mrs Mo grunted ungraciously as she planted the garland on her knobbly head.

'Coo, Coo!' laughed the doves on the buttercup branch.

> 'They don't suit you.
> Oo-hoo! Oo-hoo!'

'Meenie!' cried Mrs Mo in a rage. 'Up with you quickly and catch those birds! I'll make them into a pigeon pie!'

But the doves merely ruffled their wings and flew away, giggling.

'Two birds in the bush are worth one in the hand,' said Mr Mo, gazing after them. 'I mean,' he added nervously, 'they sing more sweetly when they're free! Don't you agree, Matilda?'

'I never agree,' snapped Mrs Mo. 'And I'll have no singing here. Mynie! Tell that man to be quiet!'

For a lusty voice was filling the air with the words of a well-known song.

'I'll sing you one-o,
Green grow the rushes-o!'

It was the Ice Cream Man, cycling along the path.

Jane and Michael had no time to wonder how he had managed to get into the little Park, for Eenie, Meenie and Mynie were shouting.

'Papa! Papa! A penny, please!'

'No ices!' bellowed Mrs Mo. 'We haven't the money to spare!'

'Matilda!' Mr Mo entreated. 'There's my lucky threepenny-piece.'

'That is for a rainy day. Not for mere enjoyment.'

'Oh, it's not going to rain, I'm sure, Matilda!'

'Of course it will rain. And, anyway, it's *my* threepenny-piece. From today, Samuel, what's yours is mine. Get along,' she yelled to the Ice Cream Man, 'and don't come here making foolish noises.'

'It's not a noise, it's a song,' he retorted. 'And I'll sing it as much as I like.'

And away he wheeled, singing

'I'll sing you two-o'

as loudly as he could.

'Out of sight,' sighed Mr Mo, as the barrow disappeared among the trees, 'but not, alas, out of mind! Well, we mustn't grumble, boys!' He brightened. 'We still have the wedding-feast. Now, Mrs Hickory, where will you sit?'

Mrs Hickory's dimples twinkled gaily.

'She won't sit anywhere, Samuel. She has not received an invitation.'

The dimples disappeared again.

'Oh, but, Matilda –!' cried Mr Mo, with a crestfallen look on his rosy face.

'But me no buts!' Mrs Mo retorted, advancing towards

the table. 'What's this?' she demanded. 'Something's missing! A peach and an orange have disappeared. And who has been eating my apple-pie?'

'I h-h-have,' said Michael nervously. 'B-but only a very small slice.'

'And I took a peach,' Jane said in a whisper. She found it hard to make the confession, Mrs Mo looked so large and fierce.

'Oh, indeed?' The knobbly woman turned to the children. 'And who invited *you*?'

'Well, you see,' began Jane. 'I was making a Park. And suddenly I found myself – I mean, it happened – I mean – I well –' However could she explain?

'Don't hum and haw, Jane, if you please. Speak when you're spoken to. Come when you're called. And, Michael, do not gape like that. The wind may change and where will you be?'

A voice that was welcome as Nuts in May sounded in their ears.

'Mary Poppins!' cried Michael in glad surprise, staring – in spite of the changing wind – from her to Mr Mo.

For there, beneath the buttercup, was the crowded perambulator. And beside it stood a tidy shape with buttoned shoes, tulip-trimmed hat and parrot-headed umbrella.

'Oh, Mary! At last! Better late than never! How are you?' cried Mr Mo. He darted round the end of the table and kissed her black-gloved hand.

'I knew he reminded me of someone!' said Michael in a careful whisper. 'Look, Jane! Their noses are just the same!'

'Nicely, thank you, Cousin Sam! My goodness, how the boys have grown!' With a ladylike air she offered her cheek to Eenie, Meenie and Mynie.

Mr Mo looked on with a fond smile. But it faded as he turned to his wife.

'And this,' he said sadly, 'is Matilda!'

Mary Poppins regarded Mrs Mo with a long and searching look. Then she smiled, to the children's great surprise, and made a dainty bow.

'I hope,' she said, in a well-bred voice, 'that we are not intruding? I wanted Sam – with your permission, of course, Matilda' – she bowed again to Mrs Mo – 'to make me a new –'

'It's ready, Mary!' cried Mr Mo, as he seized his piece of polished wood. 'All it wants is –' He flew to the perambulator. 'A nail *here* and a nail *there* and another one and it's finished!'

The brand-new handle gleamed in its place and John and Barbara clapped their hands.

'Don't think you're going to get it free!' Mrs Mo shook the rolling-pin. 'From now on, everything's got to be paid for. Nothing for nothing – that's my motto!'

'Oh, I'll certainly pay him,' said Mary Poppins, with her best society simper. 'Everyone gets what he deserves – that's my motto, Matilda!'

'Well, the quicker the better, please, Miss Poppins. I've no intention of waiting!'

'You won't have to wait, I promise you!' Mary Poppins gave a twirl to her handbag and Jane and Michael watched with interest as she glanced round the little Park. They had never seen her behave like this – such elegant tact, such polished manners.

'What a charming little place you have!' She waved the parrot-headed umbrella towards the summer-house.

Mrs Mo gave a snort of disgust.

'Charming, you call it? I call it a hovel. If Samuel thinks I can live in that, he'll have to change his mind. He's not going to knock *me* down with a feather!'

'Oh, I couldn't dream of it, Matilda! I don't possess such a thing.'

'A castle is what I want, Samuel. You owe it to your handsome bride!'

'Handsome is as handsome does!' said Mr Mo in a whisper.

But Mary Poppins' smile grew brighter.

'Handsome indeed,' she agreed admiringly. 'And you're wearing such a lovely wreath!'

'Pooh,' Mrs Mo remarked, with contempt. 'Two or three flowers twisted together. A crown of gold would be more to my liking – and I'll have it, too, before I'm finished!'

'Kind hearts are more than coronets,' said Mr Mo meekly.

'Not to me!' snapped Mrs Mo. 'I'll have a beaded band of gold! You mark my words, Miss Mary Poppins, I'll be queen of the forest yet!'

'I do not doubt it,' said Mary Poppins. And her manner was so correct and respectful that Mrs Mo smiled a mollified smile and displayed her two front teeth.

'Well,' she said grudgingly, 'now that you're here, you'd better stay and be useful. You may pass round the food at the wedding-feast. And then you can wash up the dishes.'

The children clapped their hands to their lips and glanced at Mary Poppins. What would she say to *that*? they wondered.

Mr Mo gave a gasp of horror. 'But, Matilda – don't you realize? Don't you know who she is?'

'That will do, Sam,' said Mary Poppins. She waved him aside with the parrot umbrella. Her blue eyes had grown a shade more blue, but, to Jane's and Michael's astonishment, her smile was broader than ever.

'So pleased to be of use, Matilda. And where do you plan to build your castle?'

'Well, I thought' – Mrs Mo fell back a step and swung the rolling-pin – 'we'd have the entrance gates here. And here' – she took another large stride backwards – 'the main door and the marble stairs.'

'But we can't dwell in marble halls, Matilda! They're far too grand for us.'

'For you, perhaps, Samuel. Nothing can be too grand for me. And then' – Mrs Mo fell back again – 'a large and lofty reception room where I shall receive my guests.'

'Splendid!' said Mary Poppins brightly, pushing the perambulator before her, as she followed step by step.

And behind her marched Mr Mo and the children, followed by Eenie, Meenie and Mynie, and Mrs Hickory and her babies – all of them gazing, as if in a trance, at the two figures before them.

'The ballroom here!' shouted Mrs Mo, sweeping the rolling-pin about her.

'Ballroom!' Mr Mo groaned. 'But who is going to use it?'

'I am,' said Mrs Mo, smirking. 'And you'll please let *me* do the talking, Samuel!'

'Silence is golden, Matilda, remember!' Mr Mo warned her.

'Oh, pray go on!' urged Mary Poppins, advancing another foot.

'Drawing-room! Dining-room! Pantry! Kitchen!'

Chamber by chamber the castle grew, invisible but imposing. With every word Mrs Mo fell backwards. With every word Mary Poppins stepped forward. And the rest of the party followed. They were almost across the Park now – for Mrs Mo's rooms were large and airy – and nearing the edge of the woodland.

'My bedroom will be here!' she declared, swinging her arms in a wide circle. 'And next to it' – the rolling-pin wheeled again through the air – 'I shall have a spacious nursery.'

'That will be nice for the boys, Matilda!' Mr Mo brightened at the thought.

Mrs Mo gave him a scornful glance.

'Eenie, Meenie and Mynie,' she said, 'can fend for themselves in the attic. The nursery will be for my *own* children. And – if she brings me a reference, saying she is honest and reliable – Mary Poppins may come and look after them!'

'But she's looking after us!' cried Michael. He seized a fold of the sprigged skirt and pulled her to his side.

'It's kind of you, I'm sure, Matilda. But I never give references.'

Mary Poppins' eyes had a curious glint as she thrust the perambulator forward.

'Then you're no use to me!' declared Mrs Mo, strutting backwards through her invisible mansion.

'Oh, indeed?' Mary Poppins' balmy tones had now an icy edge.

'Yes, indeed!' retorted Mrs Mo. 'I won't have people in my castle who are likely to steal the silver! And don't look at me like that!' she added. There was now a note of alarm in her voice, as though there was something frightening in the smiling face that pursued her.

'Like what?' said Mary Poppins softly. And she gave the perambulator another push.

Mrs Mo retreated again and raised her rolling-pin.

'Away with you! Be off!' she cried. 'You're an uninvited guest!' Her face was the colour of her apron and her large body trembled.

'Oh no, I'm not!' said Mary Poppins, moving forward, like an oncoming storm. 'You told me to stay and wash the dishes!'

'Well – I take it back!' quavered Mrs Mo. 'You pay us what you owe and be gone. I won't have you in my Park!'

The rolling-pin shivered in her hand as she stumbled back into the forest shade.

'*Your* Park, did you say?' murmured Mary Poppins, advancing with ever quicker steps.

'Yes, mine! Oh, Samuel, do something – can't you? I won't have her smiling at me like that! Ow! Let me go! Oh, what has caught me! I'm stuck, I can't get free! What is it?'

As she spoke, an arm went round her waist and strong hands gripped her by the wrist.

Behind her stood a stalwart figure smiling triumphantly. A head-dress of feathers was on his brow, a bow and some arrows hung from one shoulder and the other was draped with a striped blanket.

'At last! At last I find my squaw!' He grasped his wriggling captive closer.

'Let me go, you savage!' shrieked Mrs Mo, as she turned and beheld his face.

'Let go? Not I! What I find I keep. You shall come with me to my wigwam.'

'I won't! Unhand me! Samuel! Tell him to set me free!'

'Oh, I wouldn't dare – he's far too strong. And the best of friends must part, Matilda!'

'Free? Nay, nay, you shall be my slave. There!' said the Indian cheerfully, as he strung some yellow beads round her head and stuck a feather in the knob of her hair. 'This I give as a great honour. Now you're Indian too!'

'I'm not! I won't! Oh, help! Oh, Sam!'

'Well, you wanted a crown of beaded gold and you seem to have got it, my dear!'

'Wash in the stream, cook over twigs!' The Indian wrinkled his nose at her. 'All the wide greenwood for your house and sky above for your roof!'

'That's larger than the largest castle.' Mr Mo gave her a beaming glance.

'Let me go, you savage!'

'Nay, struggle not,' said the Indian, as Mrs Mo tried to wriggle away. 'A good squaw obeys her master. And a queen must do the same!'

'Queen?' cried Mrs Mo, wildly kicking.

The Indian tossed his head proudly. 'Did you not know I was King of the Forest?'

'Matilda, how splendid! Just what you wanted!'

'I didn't, I didn't! Not in this way!'

'There are more ways than one of being a queen,' said Mary Poppins primly.

Mrs Mo turned on her in a fury. She drummed with her feet on the Indian's shins and brandished the rolling-pin.

'This is *your* doing – you wolf in sheep's clothing! Things were going so nicely until you came. Oh, Samuel, why did you let her in?' Mrs Mo burst into angry tears.

'Nicely for you!' said Mary Poppins. 'But not for anyone else!'

'A wolf? A lamb, you mean, Matilda! I didn't let her in – she came. As if I could keep *that* wolf from the door!' Mr Mo laughed at his little joke.

'Oh, help me, Samuel! Set me free and I'll lend you the threepenny-piece. And the boys can have a slice of pie every second Friday!' Mrs Mo, with an imploring gesture, flung out her knobbly arms.

'What?' she cried, glaring at each in turn. 'Does *nobody* want me back?'

There was silence in the little group. Mr Mo glanced at his three sons and then at Mary Poppins. One by one all shook their heads.

> 'Coo-roo! Coo-roo!
> They don't want you!'

cooed the doves as they fluttered past.

'Oh, what shall I do?' wailed Mrs Mo.

'*I* want you, Mahtildah!' the Indian cried. 'I need you,

Mahtildah, to boil the pot! Sweep the wigwam! Sew the moccasins! Make the arrows! Fill the pipe! And – on every second Monday, Mahtildah,

> '"You shall sit on the blanket beneath a moonbeam
> And feed on wild strawberries, snakes and nut cream!"'

'Snakes? Moonbeams? Let me go! I eat nothing but mutton chops. Oh, help! Murder! Ambulance! Fire!'

Her voice rose to an anguished scream as the Indian flung her over his shoulder and stepped back into the woodland. Clasping his struggling burden tightly, he glanced at the three little boys.

'They let me go when I hollered,' he said. 'So – one good turn deserves another!'

And, smiling broadly at Mr Mo, he bore the protesting Mrs Mo into the depths of the forest.

'Police! Police!' they heard her shriek, as she and the Indian and the rolling-pin disappeared from view.

Mr Mo gave a sigh of relief.

'Well, it certainly is an ill wind that blows nobody any good! I hope Matilda will settle down and enjoy being a queen. Mary, you've paid me well for that handle. I shall always be in your debt.'

'She said she would do it in her own good time – and she has,' said Michael proudly.

'Ah!' said Mr Mo, shaking his head. 'She does everything in her own time – it's a very special kind.'

'You owe me nothing, Cousin Sam!' Mary Poppins turned away from the forest with a conquering shine in her eye. 'Except, of course,' she added severely, 'not to be so foolish in future.'

'Out of the frying-pan into the fire? Oh, I'll never marry again, Mary! Once bitten, twice shy. The boys must manage somehow.'

'Perhaps, Mr Mo,' Mrs Hickory dimpled, 'you would let *me* wash and mend for them. It would be no trouble at all.'

'What a beautiful thought!' cried Mr Mo. 'All's well that ends well, Mary, you see! And I in return, Mrs Hickory, will build you a nice little house. Oh, I've lost sixpence and found a shilling! Look!' he said, pointing to the sunset. 'Red sky at night is the shepherd's delight! My dears, we are all going to be so happy. I shall start on my Fun Fair at once!'

And away he dashed across the lawn, with the rest of the party at his heels.

'But what about the wedding-breakfast?' Michael panted after him.

'My goodness, I'd forgotten. Here – fruit, cake, sausages, buns!' He took a piece from every dish and thrust it into Michael's hands.

Mary Poppins looked on disapprovingly.

'Now, Michael, not another bite! You will have no room for your supper.'

'Enough's as good as a feast, my lad!' Mr Mo grinned at Michael as he watched the food disappearing.

'Enough is too much!' said Mary Poppins. 'Come along, both of you!'

'Oh, I cannot bear to leave it!' cried Jane. Her little Park seemed brighter than ever, as it shone in the setting sun.

'You never will!' Mr Mo declared. 'As long as you remember it, you can always come and go. And I hope you're not going to tell me that you can't be in two places at once. A clever girl who makes parks and people surely knows how to do that!' He smiled his twinkling, teasing smile.

Mary Poppins stepped out from under the buttercup, with a homeward look in her eye.

'Say good-bye politely, Jane!' She sent the perambulator rolling along the pebbled path.

'Good-bye, Mr Mo!' said Jane softly, as she stood on tip-toe and held out her arms.

'Oh, luck! Oh, joy!' He patted his cheek. 'This is no Park for Poor People! I'm rich – she's given me a kiss! Share and share alike!' he cried, as he kissed Mrs Hickory right on a dimple.

'Remember, Sam!' warned Mary Poppins. 'Look before you leap!'

'Oh, I shan't do any leaping, Mary! A little dance and a hop or two – nothing more serious, I assure you!'

She gave a disbelieving sniff, but Mr Mo did not hear it. He was skipping beside Mrs Hickory and seizing her apron-strings.

'May I have the pleasure?' they heard him saying.

'Me, too!' cried Eenie, Meenie and Mynie, as they flew to join their father.

And there they all were, prancing round the table, helping themselves to pie and wine and hanging the cherries behind their ears. Mrs Hickory's dimples were twinkling gaily and her babies were bobbing about in her arms.

'It's a poor heart that never rejoices!' cried Mr Mo, as he whirled her about. He seemed to have quite forgotten his guests in the gaiety of the moment.

'It's love that makes the world go round!' yelled Eenie, Meenie and Mynie.

And, indeed, the world did seem to be spinning, turning for joy upon its axis, as the little Park spun round its buttercup tree. Round and round and round it went in a steady, stately movement.

The wedding-party was waltzing and singing, and the Ice Cream Man was singing, too, as he pedalled back along the path. A cluster of Fruit Bars was in his hand and he tossed them on to the table.

'Three for luck and free for luck!' he cried, as he trundled by.

'Step up, if you please,' said Mary Poppins, hustling them along before her as a hen hustles her chicks. 'And what are you doing, Jane and Michael, walking backwards like that?'

'I'b wadching the weddig-feast!' mumbled Michael, with his mouth full of his last cherry. He gave a long, lugubrious sigh as each creak of the perambulator drew him farther from that wonderful meal.

'Taking one more look at my Park, Mary Poppins,' said Jane, as she gazed at the happy scene.

'Well, you're not a pair of crabs! Turn round – and walk in the right direction.'

The sunset dazzled their eyes as they turned. And the afternoon seemed to be turning with them, from two o'clock till five. Tick-tock! said every clock. Ding-dong! said the bells in the steeples.

Then the spinning world slowed down and was still, and they blinked as though coming out of a dream. Had it taken them seconds, minutes or hours to walk down that pebbly path? They looked about them curiously.

The blossoms of clover were now at their feet, instead of above their heads, and the grasses of the Wild Corner brushed against their knees. The bumble-bee went buzzing by, no larger, it seemed, than usual. And the fly on a near-by bluebell was about the size of a fly. As for that ant – it was hiding under a grass-seed and was therefore invisible.

The big Park spread serenely round them, just the same as ever. The Ice Cream Man, who had come to the last verse of his song –

> 'I'll sing you twelve-o
> Green grow the rushes-o,'

171

was wheeling away from the Wild Corner. And the Park Keeper, with the finished daisy-chain round his neck, was lumbering towards them.

They glanced down. Below them lay the little Park, hemmed in by its walls of weed. They blinked again and smiled at each other as they fell on their knees among the flowers.

The little lawns were now in shadow. Long patterns of daisy and bluebell lay black across the paths. The tiny flowers in Jane's garden were bending on their stems. By lake and swing the seats were deserted.

'They've eaten every bit of the feast. Look!' whispered Michael. 'Empty plates!'

'And not a sign of anyone. I expect they've all gone home to bed.' Jane sighed. She would like to have seen Mr Mo again, and to measure herself against his elbow.

'They're lucky, then, 'ooever they are! Let's to bed, says Sleepy-'Ead – as they told me when I was a boy!' The Park Keeper stooped above them and surveyed Jane's handiwork.

'No Parks allowed in the Park!' he observed. Then he eyed the two rapt faces. 'Well, you seem very pre-h'occupied! What are you lookin' for?'

Jane gave him an absent-minded glance.

'Mary Poppins' cousin,' she murmured, as she searched through the little Park.

The Park Keeper's face was a sight to see.

'Cousin! Down there – among the weeds? You'll be tellin' me next 'e's a beetle!'

'*I'll* be telling you something in a minute!' said a wrathful voice beside him. Mary Poppins regarded him frostily. 'Did I or didn't I hear you referring to me as an insect?'

'Well – not to you,' the Park Keeper faltered. 'But if your cousin's down in that grass, what can 'e be but a beetle?'

'Oh, indeed! And if he's a beetle, what am I?'

He looked at her uneasily and wished that something would strike him dumb.

'Hum,' he said, fumbling for a word. 'I may be as mad as a March Hatter –'

'*May* be!' she gave a disdainful sniff.

'But I don't see 'ow you *can* 'ave a cousin sittin' under a buttercup!'

'I can have a cousin anywhere – and no business of yours!'

'You can't!' he cried. 'T'isn't natural. I suppose,' he added sarcastically, 'you're related to the Man in the Moon!'

'My uncle!' said Mary Poppins calmly, as she turned the perambulator into the path that led from the Wild Corner.

The Park Keeper opened his mouth in surprise and shut it again with a snap.

'Ha, ha! You will 'ave your little joke. 'Owsumever, I don't believe it!'

'Nobody asked you to,' she replied. 'Come, Jane! Come, Michael! Quick march, please!'

Night had now come to the little Park. The wildweed, thickly clustered about it, looked very like a forest. No light came through the trackless stems, it was dark as any jungle. With a last glance at the lonely lawns, they turned away regretfully and ran after the perambulator.

'Mary Poppins! They've all gone home,' cried Michael. 'There's nothing left on the plates.'

'East, West, home's best. And who are "they", I'd like to know?'

'I meant your funny little cousin – and all his family!'

She pulled up sharply and looked at him with a calm that was worse than anger.

'Did you say "funny"?' she inquired. 'And what was so funny about him, pray?'

'Well – at first he wasn't as big as a beetle and then he stretched out to the usual s-s-size!' He trembled as he looked at her.

'Beetles again! Why not grasshoppers? Or perhaps you'd prefer a grub! Stretching, indeed! Are you trying to tell me, Michael Banks, that my cousin is made of elastic?'

'Well – no, not elastic. Plasticine!' There! It was out. He had said it at last.

She drew herself up. And now it seemed as if *she* were stretching, for her rage seemed to make her twice as tall.

'Well!' she began, in a voice that told him clearly she had never been so shocked in her life. 'If anyone had ever warned me –' But he interrupted wildly.

'Oh, don't be angry, *please*, Mary Poppins – not in your tulip hat! I didn't mean he was funny to laugh at, but funny in the nicest way. And I won't say another word – I promise!'

'Humph!' She subsided. 'Silence is golden.'

And as she stalked along beside him, with her heels going click-clack on the path, he wondered where he had heard that before.

He glanced at Jane carefully from the corner of his eye.

'But it happened, didn't it?' he whispered. 'We did go into the little Park and join them at the feast? I'm sure it was true, because I'm not hungry. All I want for supper is a hard-boiled egg and a piece of buttered toast. And rice pudding and two tomatoes and perhaps a cup of milk!'

'Oh, yes, it was true.' Jane sighed for joy as she gazed round the great familiar Park. Within it, she knew, lay another one. And perhaps –

'Do you think, Mary Poppins –' She hesitated. 'Do you think that everything in the world is inside something else? My little Park inside a big one and the big one inside a larger one? Again and again? Away and away?' She waved

her arm to take in the sky. 'And to someone very far out there – do you think we would look like ants?'

'Ants and beetles! Grasshoppers! Grubs! What next, I'd like to know! I can't answer for you, Jane, but *I'm* not an ant to *anyone*, thank you!'

Mary Poppins gave a disgusted sniff.

'Of course you're not!' said a cheerful voice, as Mr Banks – coming back from the City – caught up with the little group.

'You're more like a glow-worm, Mary Poppins, shining to show us the right way home!' He waited for the self-satisfied smile to spread across her face. 'Here,' he said, 'take the evening paper and I'll wheel the perambulator. The exercise will do me good. I think I'm getting a cold.'

The Twins and Annabel crowed with delight as Mr Banks sent them skimming along.

'Dear me,' he remarked. 'What a fine new handle! That cousin of yours is a good workman. You must let me know what you paid for it.'

'*I* know!' cried Michael eagerly. 'She gave Mrs Mo to the Indian!'

'Atishoo! I didn't quite hear what you said, Michael. She gave Mr Rowe two shillings?' Mr Banks blew his nose with a flourish.

'No, no! She gave Mrs Mo –! I mean –' He never finished the sentence. For Mary Poppins' eye was on him and he thought it best to drop the subject.

'There will be no charge, sir!' she said politely. 'My cousin was pleased to do it.'

'That's uncommonly kind of him, Mary Poppins. Hey!' he broke off. 'Do look where you're going! Observe the rules of the Park, Smith! You nearly upset the per-ambulator.'

For the Park Keeper, bounding after them, had knocked into the little group and scattered it in all directions.

'Beg pardon all, I'm sure!' he panted. 'Sorry, Mr Banks, sir, but if you'll excuse me, it's *'er* I'm after.'

He flung out a hand at Mary Poppins. The daisy-chain dangled from his wrist.

'Why, Mary Poppins, what have you done? Broken a bye-law or what?'

The Park Keeper gave a lonely groan.

'Bye-law? She's broken *all* the laws! Oh, it isn't natural - but it's true!' He turned to Mary Poppins.

'You said you could 'ave one anywhere! Well, 'e's down there under a dandelion. I 'eard 'im with me own ears – laughin' and singin' – just like a party. 'Ere, take it!' he cried in a broken voice, as he flung the daisy-chain over her head. 'I meant it for me poor old mother – but I feel I owe you somethin'.'

'You do,' said Mary Poppins calmly, as she straightened the daisy-chain.

The Park Keeper stared at her for a moment. Then he turned away with a sigh.

'I shall never h'understand,' he muttered, knocking over a litter-basket as he tottered off down the path.

Mr Banks gazed after him with a look of shocked surprise.

'Somebody under a dandelion? Having a party? What can he mean? Really, I sometimes wonder if Smith is right in the head. Under a dandelion – laughing and singing! Did you ever hear such a thing?'

'Never!' said Mary Poppins demurely, with a dainty shake of her head.

And as she shook it a buttercup petal fell from the brim of her hat.

The children watched it fluttering down and turned and smiled at each other.

'There's one on your head, too, Michael!'

'Is there?' he said, with a happy sigh. 'Bend down and let me look at yours.'

And, sure enough, Jane had a petal, too.

'I told you so!' She nodded wisely. And she held her head very high and still so as not to disturb it.

Crowned with the gold of the buttercup tree, she walked home under the maple boughs. All was quiet. The sun had set. The shadows of the Long Walk were falling all about her. And at the same time the brightness of the little Park folded her closely round. The dark of one, the light of the other – she felt them both together.

'I am in two places at once,' she whispered, 'just as he said I would be!'

And she thought again of the little clearing among the thronging weeds. The daisies would grow again, she knew. Clover would hide the little lawns. Cardboard table and swings would crumble. The forest would cover it all.

But somehow, somewhere, in spite of that, she knew she would find it again – as neat and as gay and as happy as it had been today. She only had to remember it and there she would be once more. Time upon time she would return – hadn't Mr Mo said so? – and stand at the edge of that patch of brightness and never see it fade . . .

CHAPTER SIX

Hallowe'en

'Mary Poppins!' called Michael. 'Wait for us!'

'W-a-a-a-i-t!' the wind echoed, whining round him.

It was a dusky, gusty autumn evening. The clouds blew in and out of the sky. And in all the houses of Cherry Tree Lane the curtains blew in and out of the windows. Swish-swish. Flap-flap.

The Park was tossing like a ship in a storm. Leaves and litter-paper turned head-over-heels in the air. The trees groaned and waved their arms, the spray of the fountain was blown and scattered. Benches shivered. Swings were creaking. The Lake water leapt into foamy waves. Nothing was still in the whole Park as it bowed and shuddered under the wind.

And through it all stalked Mary Poppins, with not a hair out of place. Her neat blue coat with its silver buttons was neither creased nor ruffled, and the tulip sat on her hat so firmly that it might have been made of marble.

Far behind her the children ran, splashing through drifts of leaves. They had been to Mr Folly's stall for nuts and toffee-apples. And now they were trying to catch her up.

'*Wait for us, Mary Poppins!*'

In front of her, on the Long Walk, the perambulator trundled. The wind whistled through the wheels, and the Twins and Annabel clung together for fear of being blown

179

overboard. Their tasselled caps were tossing wildly and the rug was flapping loose, like a flag.

'O-o-o-h!' they squeaked, like excited mice, as a sudden gust tore it free and carried it away.

Someone was coming down the path, bowling along like a tattered newspaper.

'Help!' shrilled a high, familiar voice. 'Something has blown right over my hat! I can't see where I'm going.'

It was Miss Lark, out for her evening walk. Her two dogs bounded on ahead and behind her the Professor straggled, with his hair standing on end.

'Is that you, Mary Poppins?' she cried, as she plucked the rug away from her face and flung it upon the perambulator. 'What a dreadful night! Such a wild wind! I wonder you're not blown away!'

Mary Poppins raised her eyebrows and gave a superior sniff. If the wind blew anyone away, it would not be herself, she thought.

'What do you mean – a dreadful night?' Admiral Boom strode up behind them. His dachshund, Pompey, was at his heels, wearing a little sailor's jacket to keep him from catching cold.

'It's a perfect night, my dear lady, for a life on the ocean wave!

> "Sixteen men on a dead man's chest –
> Yo, ho, ho! And a bottle of rum."

You must sail the Seven Seas, Lucinda!'

'Oh – I couldn't sit on a dead man's chest!' Miss Lark seemed quite upset at the thought. 'Nor drink rum, either, Admiral. Do keep up, Professor, please. There – my scarf has blown away! Oh, goodness, now the dogs have gone!'

'Perhaps they've blown away, too!' The Professor glanced up into a tree, looking for Andrew and Willoughby. Then he peered short-sightedly down the Walk.

'Ah, here they come!' he murmured vaguely. 'How strange they look with only two legs!'

'Two legs!' said Miss Lark reproachfully. 'How absent-minded you are, Professor. Those aren't my darling precious dogs – they're only Jane and Michael.'

The Admiral whipped out his telescope and clapped it to his eye.

'Ahoy, there, shipmates!' he roared to the children.

'Look!' shouted Michael, running up. 'I put out my hand to hold my cap and the wind blew a leaf right into it!'

'And one into mine the same minute!' Jane panted behind him.

They stood there, laughing and glowing, with their packages held against their chests and the star-shaped maple leaves in their hands.

'Thank you,' said Mary Poppins firmly, as she plucked

the leaves from between their fingers, gave them a scrutinizing glance and popped them into her pocket.

'Catch a leaf, a message brief!' Miss Lark's voice shrieked above the wind. 'But, of course, it's only an old wives' tale. Ah, there you are, dear dogs – at last! Take my hand, Professor, please. We must hurry home to safety.'

And she shooed them all along before her, with her skirts blowing out in every direction.

Michael hopped excitedly. 'Was it a message, Mary Poppins?'

'That's as may be,' said Mary Poppins, turning up her nose to the sky.

'But we caught them!' Jane protested.

'C. caught it. G. got it,' she answered, with annoying calm.

'Will you show us when we get home?' screamed Michael, his voice floating away.

'Home is the sailor, home from the sea!' The Admiral took off his hat with a flourish. 'Au revoir, messmates and Miss Poppins! Up with the anchor, Pompey!'

'Ay, ay, sir!' Pompey seemed to be saying, as he galloped after his master.

Michael rummaged in his package.

'Mary Poppins, why didn't you wait? I wanted to give you a toffee-apple.'

'Time and tide wait for no man,' she answered priggishly.

He was just about to ask what time and tide had to do with toffee-apples, when he caught her disapproving look.

'A pair of Golliwogs – that's what you are! Just look at your hair! Sweets to the sweet,' she added conceitedly, as she took the sticky fruit he offered and nibbled it daintily.

'It's not our fault, it's the wind!' said Michael, tossing the hair from his brow.

'Well, the quicker you're into it the quicker you're out

of it!' She thrust the perambulator forward under the groaning trees.

'Look out! Be careful! What are you doin'?'

A howl of protest rent the air as a figure, clutching his tie and his cap, lurched sideways in the dusk.

'Remember the bye-laws! Look where you're goin'! You can't knock over the Park Keeper.'

Mary Poppins gave him a haughty stare.

'I can if he's in my way,' she retorted. 'You'd no right to be there.'

'I've a right to be anywhere in the Park. It's in the Regulations.' He peered at her through the gathering dark and staggered back with a cry.

'Toffee-apples? And bags o'nuts? Then it must be 'Allowe'en! I might 'ave known it –' His voice shook. 'You don't get a wind like this for nothin'. O-o-ow!' He shuddered. 'It gives me the 'Orrors. I'll leave the Park to look after itself. This is no night to be out.'

'Why not?' Jane handed him a nut. 'What happens at Hallowe'en?'

The Park Keeper's eyes grew as round as plates. He glanced nervously over his shoulder and leant towards the children.

'*Things*,' he said in a hoarse whisper, 'come out and walk in the night. I don't know what they are quite – never 'avin' seen them – ghosts, perhaps, or h'apparitions. Anyway, it's spooky. Hey – what's that?' He clutched his stick. 'Look! There's one of them up there – a white thing in the trees!'

A light was gleaming among the branches, turning their black to silver. The wind had blown the clouds away and a great bright globe rode through the sky.

'It's only the moon!' Jane and Michael laughed. 'Don't you recognize it?'

'Ah –' The Park Keeper shook his head. 'It *looks* like

the moon and it *feels* like the moon. And it may be the moon – *but it may not*. You never can tell on 'Allowe'en!'

And he turned up his coat-collar and hurried away, not daring to look behind him.

'Of course it's the moon,' said Michael stoutly. 'There's moonlight on the grass!'

Jane gazed at the glowing, shining scene.

'The bushes are dancing in the wind. Look! There's one coming towards us – a small bush and two larger ones. Oh, Mary Poppins, perhaps they're ghosts?' She clutched a fold of the blue coat. 'They're coming nearer, Mary Poppins! I'm sure they're apparitions!'

'I don't want to see them!' Michael screamed. He seized the end of the parrot umbrella as though it were an anchor.

'Apparitions, indeed!' shrieked the smallest bush. 'Well, I've heard myself called many things – Charlemagne said I looked like a fairy and Boadicea called me a goblin – but nobody ever said to my face that I was an apparition. Though I dare say' – the bush gave a witch-like cackle – 'that I often look like one!'

A skinny little pair of legs came capering towards them and a wizened face, like an old apple, peered out through wisps of hair.

Michael drew a long breath.

'It's only Mrs Corry!' he said, loosing his hold on the parrot umbrella.

'And Miss Fannie and Miss Annie!' Jane waved in relief to the two large bushes.

'How de do?' said their mournful voices, as Mrs Corry's enormous daughters caught up with their tiny mother.

'Well, here we are again, my dears – as I heard St George remark to the Dragon. Just the kind of night for –' Mrs Corry looked at Mary Poppins and gave her a knowing

grin. 'For all sorts of
things,' she concluded.
'You got a message, I
hope!'

'Thank you kindly, Mrs
Corry. I have had a com-
munication.'

'What message?' asked
Michael inquisitively. 'Was
it one on a leaf?'

Mrs Corry cocked her
head. And her coat – which
was covered with three-
penny bits – twinkled in the moonlight.

'Ah,' she murmured mysteriously. 'There are so many
kinds of communication! You look at me, I look at you,
and something passes between us. John o' Groats could
send me a message, simply by dropping an eyelid. And
once – five hundred years ago – Mother Goose handed me
a feather. I knew exactly what it meant – "Come to dinner,
Roast Duck"!'

'And a tasty dish it must have been! But, excuse me,
Mrs Corry, please – we must be getting home. This is no
night for dawdling – as you will understand.' Mary Poppins gave her a meaning look.

'Quite right, Miss Poppins! Early to bed, early to rise,
makes a man healthy, wealthy and – Now, who was it first
told me that – Robert the Bruce? No, I've forgotten!'

'See you later,' said Fannie and Annie, waving to Jane
and Michael.

'Later?' said Jane. 'But we're going to bed.'

'There you go – you galumphing giraffes! Can't you
ever open your mouths without putting your feet into
them? They mean, my dears,' said Mrs Corry, 'they'll be
seeing you later in the *year*! November, perhaps, or after

Christmas. Unless, of course' – her smile widened – 'unless you are *very clever*! Well, good night and sleep well!'

She held out her little wrinkled hands and Jane and Michael both sprang forward.

'Look out! Look out!' she shrieked at them. 'You're stepping on my shadow!'

'Oh – I'm sorry!' They both jumped back in alarm.

'Deary goodness – you gave me a turn!' Mrs Corry clapped her hand to her heart. 'Two of you standing right on its head – the poor thing *will* be distressed!'

They looked at her in astonishment and then at the little patch of black that lay on the windy grass.

'But I didn't think shadows could feel,' said Jane.

'Not feel! What nonsense!' cried Mrs Corry. 'They feel twice as much as you do. I warn you, children, take care of your shadows or your shadows won't take care of you. How would you like to wake one morning and find they had run away? And what's a man without a shadow? Practically nothing, you might say!'

'I wouldn't like it at all,' said Michael, glancing at his own shadow rippling in the wind. He realized, for the first

time, how fond he was of it.

'Exactly!' Mrs Corry snorted. 'Ah, my love,' she crooned to her shadow. 'We've been through a lot together – haven't we? – you and I. And never a hair of your head hurt till these two went and stepped on it. All right, all right, don't look so glum!' She twinkled at Jane and Michael. 'But remember what I say – take care! Fannie and Annie, stir your stumps. Look lively – if you possibly can!'

And off she trotted between her daughters, bending sideways now and again to blow a kiss to her shadow.

'Now, come along. No loitering,' said Mary Poppins briskly.

'We're keeping an eye on our shadows!' said Jane. 'We don't want anything to hurt them.'

'You and your shadows,' said Mary Poppins, 'can go to bed – spit-spot!'

And, sure enough, that was what they did. In next to no time they had eaten their supper, undressed before the crackling fire and bounced under the blankets.

The nursery curtains blew in and out and the night-light flickered on the ceiling.

'I see my shadow and my shadow sees me!' Jane looked at the neatly brushed head reflected on the wall. She nodded in a friendly way and her shadow nodded back.

'My shadow and I are two swans!' Michael held his arm in the air and snapped his fingers together. And upon the wall a long-necked bird opened and closed its beak.

'Swans!' said Mary Poppins, sniffing, as she laid her coat and tulip hat at the end of her camp-bed. 'Geese more like it, *I* should say!'

The canvas creaked as she sprang in.

Michael craned his neck and called: 'Why don't you hang up your coat, Mary Poppins, the way you always do?'

'My feet are cold, that's why! Now, not another word!'

He looked at Jane. Jane looked at him. They knew it was only half an answer. What was she up to tonight? They wondered. But Mary Poppins never explained. You might as well ask the Sphinx.

'Tick!' said the clock on the mantelpiece.

They were warm as toast inside their beds. And their

beds were warm inside the nursery. And the nursery was warm inside the house. And the howling of the wind outside made it seem warmer still.

They leaned their cheeks upon their palms and let their eyelids fall.

'Tock!' said the clock on the mantelpiece.

But neither of them heard . . .

'What is it?' Jane murmured sleepily. 'Who's scratching my nose?'

'It's me!' said Michael in a whisper. He was standing at the side of her bed with a wrinkled leaf in his hand.

'I've been scratching it for ages, Jane! The front door banged and woke me up and I found this on my pillow. Look! There's one on yours, too. And Mary Poppins' bed is empty and her coat and hat have gone!'

Jane took the leaves and ran to the window.

'Michael,' she cried, 'there *was* a message. One leaf says "Come" and the other "Tonight".'

'But where has she gone? I can't see her!' He craned his neck and looked out.

All was quiet. The wind had dropped. Every house was fast asleep. And the full moon filled the world with light.

'Jane! There are shadows in the garden – and not a single person!'

He pointed to two little dark shapes – one in pyjamas, one in a nightgown – that were floating down the front path and through the garden railings.

Jane glanced at the nursery walls and ceiling. The nightlight glowed like a bright eye. But in spite of that steady, watchful gleam there was not a single shadow!

'They're ours, Michael! Put something on. Quick – we must go and catch them!'

He seized a sweater and followed her, tiptoeing down the creaking stairs and out into the moonlight.

Cherry Tree Lane was calm and still, but from the Park came strains of music and trills of high-pitched laughter.

The children, clutching their brown leaves, dashed through the Lane Gate. And something, light as snow or feathers, fell upon Michael's shoulder. Something gentler than air brushed against Jane's cheek.

'Touched you last!' two voices cried. And they turned and beheld their shadows.

'But why did you run away?' asked Jane, gazing at the transparent face that looked so like her own.

'We're guests at the Party.' Her shadow smiled.

'What party?' Michael demanded.

'It's Hallowe'en,' his shadow told him. 'The night when every shadow is free. And this is a very special occasion. For one thing, there's a full moon – and it falls on the Birthday Eve. But come along, we mustn't be late!'

And away the two little shadows flitted, with the children solidly running behind them.

The music grew louder every second, and as they darted round the laurels they beheld a curious sight.

The whole playground was thronged with shadows, each of them laughing and greeting the others and hopping about in the moonlight. And the strange thing was that, instead of lying flat on the ground, they were all standing upright. Long shadows, short shadows, thin shadows, fat shadows, were bobbing, hobnobbing, bowing, kowtowing, and passing in and out of each other with happy cries of welcome.

In one of the swings sat a helmeted shape, playing a concertina. It smiled and waved a shadowy hand, and Jane and Michael saw at once that it belonged to the Policeman.

'Got your invitations?' he cried. 'No human beings allowed in without a special pass!'

Jane and Michael held up their leaves.

'Good!' The Policeman's shadow nodded. 'Bless you!' he added, as a shape beside him was seized with a fit of sneezing.

Could it be Ellen's shadow? Yes – and blowing a shadowy nose!

'Good evening!' murmured a passing shape, 'if any evening's good!'

Its dreary voice and long face reminded Jane of the Fishmonger. And surely the jovial shadow beside it belonged to the Family Butcher! A shadowy knife was in his hand, a striped apron about his waist, and he led along an airy figure with horns upon its head.

'Michael!' said Jane in a loud whisper. 'I think that's the Dancing Cow!'

But Michael was too absorbed to answer. He was chatting to a furry shape that was lazily trimming its whiskers.

'My other part,' it said, miaowing, 'is asleep on the mantelpiece. So, of course – this being Hallowe'en – I took the evening off!' It adjusted a shadowy wreath of flowers that was looped about its neck.

'The Cat that looked at the King!' exclaimed Jane. She put out a hand to stroke its head, but all she felt was the air.

'Well, don't let him come near me!' cried a voice. 'I've quite enough troubles as it is, without having cats to deal with.'

A plump, bird-like shape tripped past, nodding abstractedly at the children.

'Poor old Cock Robin – and his troubles!' The shadowy Cat gave a shadowy yawn. 'He's never got over that funeral and all the fuss there was.'

'Cock Robin? But he's a Nursery Rhyme. He doesn't exist!' said Jane.

'Doesn't exist? Then why am *I* here?' The phantom bird seemed quite annoyed. 'You can have a substance without a shadow, but you can't have a shadow without a substance – anyone knows that! And what about them – don't *they* exist?'

It waved a dark transparent wing at a group of airy figures – a tall boy lifting a flute to his mouth, and a bulky shape, with a crown on its head, clasping a bowl and a pipe. Beside them stood three phantom fiddlers holding their bows aloft.

A peal of laughter burst from Michael. 'That's the shadow of Old King Cole. It's exactly like the picture!'

'And Tom, the Piper's son, too!' Cock Robin glared at Jane. 'If they're shadows, they must be shadows of *something* – deny it if you can!'

'Balloons *and* balloons, my deary ducks! No arguing tonight!' A cosy little feminine shape, with balloons bobbing about her bonnet, whizzed through the air above them.

'Have the goodness, please, to be more careful. You nearly went through my hat!'

A trumpeting voice that was somehow familiar sounded amid the laughter. The children peered through the weaving crowd. Could it be? – yes, it was – Miss Andrew! Or rather, Miss Andrew's shadow. The same beaked nose, the same small eyes, the grey veil over the felt hat and the coat of rabbit fur.

'I haven't come from the South Seas to have my head knocked off!'

Shaking its fist at the Balloon Woman, Miss Andrew's shadow protested loudly. 'And who's that pulling my veil?'

it cried, turning on two little dark shapes, who dashed away, screaming with terror.

Jane and Michael nudged each other. 'Ours!' they whispered, giggling.

'Make way! Move on! The Prime Minister's comin'!' A shadow in a peaked cap waved the children aside.

'Oh, it's you, is it? Well, remember the bye-laws! Don't get in anyone's way.' The phantom face – the moustache and all – was exactly like the Park Keeper's.

'I thought you'd have been too frightened to come. You said it was spooky!' Jane reminded him.

'Oh, I'm not frightened, Miss – it's 'im. My body, so to speak. A very nervous chap 'e is – afraid of 'is own shadow Ha, ha! Excuse my little joke! Make room! Move on! Observe the rules!'

The Prime Minister's shadow floated by, bowing to right and left.

'Greeting, friends! What a wonderful night. Dear me!' He stared at Jane and Michael. 'You're very thick and lumpish!'

'Hsssst!' The shadow of the Park Keeper muttered in his ear. 'Invitation . . . special occasion . . . friends of . . . whisper, whisper.'

'Ah! If that's the case, you're very welcome. But do be careful where you tread. We don't like to be stepped on.'

'One of them's stepping on me, I think!' A nervous voice seemed to come from the grass.

Michael carefully shifted his feet as the shadow of the Keeper of the Zoological Gardens came crawling past on all fours.

'Any luck?' cried the crowd excitedly.

'Hundreds!' came the happy reply. 'Red Admirals. Blue Admirals. Spotted Bermudas. Pink Amazons. Chinese Yellows!'

He waved the shadow of his net. It was full of butterfly shadows.

'Well, I know one you haven't got – and that's an Admiral Boom!' A shadow in a cocked hat, with a spectral dachshund at its heels, elbowed its way through the throng. 'Very rare specimen indeed. Largest butterfly in the world! All hail, my hearties!'

'Yo, ho, ho! And a bottle of rum!' The shadows yelled in reply.

The Admiral's shadow turned to the children.

'Welcome aboard!' it said, winking. '"Catch a leaf, a message brief" – only an old wives' tale – hey? Ah, here she comes! Your servant, ma'am.'

The cocked hat bowed to a broad shadow that was sailing through the see-saw. It was dressed in a shadowy swirl of skirts, and a swarm of little weightless shapes fluttered about its head.

'The Bird Woman!' whispered Jane to Michael.

'Who are you callin' an old wife? Feed the birds! Tuppence a bag!'

A cry of pleasure went up from the crowd as everyone greeted the new arrival. The children saw their own reflections running to kiss her cheeks, and as though – tonight – *they* were the shadows, they hurried after them.

The party was growing more and more lively. The whole Park was ringing with laughter. And above the voices, high and sweet, came the reedy note of the flute.

'Over the hills and far away!' played Tom, the Piper's Son.

And in Cherry Tree Lane the people lying in bed listened and huddled under the blankets.

'It's Hallowe'en!' each said to himself. 'Of course I don't believe in ghosts – but listen to them shrieking!'

They would have been surprised, perhaps, had they dared to look out of the window.

Every second the crowd thickened. And it seemed to the children as they watched that everyone they had ever known had a shadow at the party. Was that Aunt Flossie's? They could not tell. She was there and gone again. And surely those were John's and Barbara's flitting among the leaves!

'Well, lovies?' murmured the Bird Woman's shadow, as it smiled at the four young faces – a girl with her airy shape beside her and a boy arm-in-arm with his double.

'Quack-quack!' said a voice at the same moment.

'Oh, Goosey-Gander, wait for us!' And away went the airy children.

The Bird Woman's shadow gathered its skirts and made room on the bench for Jane and Michael.

'My!' she exclaimed, as her arms went round them. 'You're solid and no mistake!'

'That's because we're real,' said Jane.

'Bones and toe-nails and hair and blood,' Michael kindly informed her.

'Ah!' The Bird Woman's shadow nodded. 'I expect you 'ad a Special Ticket. It isn't everyone gets the chance. But you're not tellin' me – are you, lovies? – that shadders isn't real?'

'Well – they go through things. And they're made of nothing –' Jane tried to explain.

The Bird Woman shook her shadowy head.

'Nothin's made of nothin', lovey. And that's what they're for – to go through things. Through and out on the other side – it's the way they get to be wise. You take my word for it, my loves, when you know what your shadder knows – then you know a lot. Your shadder's the other part of you, the outside of your inside – if you understand what I mean.'

'Don't explain! It's no use. *They* don't understand anything!'

The portly shadow of Cock Robin came tripping past the bench.

'They told me only a moment ago that Cock Robin never existed. Well, who was buried, I'd like to know! And why were the birds a-sighing and a-sobbing? Take care, Bo-peep! Do look where you're going. Those lambs of yours nearly knocked me over!'

A shadow carrying a crook was skimming through the crowd. And behind her a flock of curly shapes gambolled on the lawn.

'But I thought Bo-peep had *lost* her sheep!' cried Michael in surprise.

'That's right!' The Bird Woman's shadow chuckled. 'But 'er shadder always finds them.'

'We've been looking for you everywhere!' a trio of voices grunted. Three furry shadows scattered the sheep and bore Bo-peep away.

'Oh!' exclaimed Jane. 'They're the Three Bears. I hope they'll do nothing to hurt her.'

'Hurt her? Bless you, why should they? A shadder never did anyone harm – at least, not as I know of. See! The four of 'em – dancin' together as friendly as can be!'

The Bird Woman's shadow surveyed the scene, beating time to the Piper's flute. Then suddenly the music changed and she started up with a cry. ''Ere they are at last, lovies! Get up on the bench and look!'

'Who are here?' demanded Michael. But even as he spoke, he knew.

The music of the concertina had changed to a stately

march. The shadows were clearing a path in their midst.
And down between the waving lines came a pair of familiar
figures.

One of them was small and old, with elastic-sided boots
on her feet and threepenny bits on her coat.

And the other – oh, how well they knew it – was carrying a
parrot-headed umbrella and wearing a tulip-trimmed hat.

Tum! Tum! Tee-um, tum, tum! the concertina
boomed.

On they came, the two figures, graciously bowing to all
spectators and followed by the bulky forms of Fannie and
Annie Corry. Solid flesh and bone they were amid the
transparent shapes, and the children saw that their four
shadows were firmly attached to their heels.

A shout of rapture rose from the throng.

And the sleepers in Cherry Tree Lane shuddered and
thrust their heads under their pillows.

'A Hallowe'en welcome, Mary Poppins! Three cheers
for the Birthday Eve!'

' 'Ip, 'Ip, 'Ooray!' yelled the Bird Woman's shadow.

'Whose birthday is it?' Jane inquired. She was standing
on tiptoe on the bench, trembling with excitement.

'It's 'ers – Miss Mary Poppins' – tomorrer! 'Allowe'en
falls on the day before, so of course we make a night of it.
Feed the Birds! Tuppence a bag!' she shouted to Mary
Poppins.

The rosy face beneath the tulip smiled at her in ac-
knowledgement. Then it glanced up at the two children
and the smile disappeared.

'Why aren't you wearing a dressing-gown, Michael?
And, Jane, where are your slippers? A fine pair of scare-
crows you are – to come to an evening party!'

'Aha! You were cleverer than I thought! Taking care of
your shadows, I hope!' Mrs Corry grinned.

But before the children had time to reply, the music

The shadows were clearing a path in their midst

changed from a solemn march to a reeling, romping dance.

'Choose your partners! Time's running out! We must all be back on the stroke of twelve!' The voice of the Policeman's shadow rose above the laughter.

'Pray give me the pleasure, dearest friend!' The shadow of the Father Bear bowed to Mrs Corry.

'A-a-way, you rolling river!' The Admiral's shadow grasped Miss Andrew's and whirled it through a litter-basket.

The Fishmonger's shadow raised its hat to another that looked like Mrs Brill; the shadow of the Mother Bear floated to Old King Cole. The Prime Minister's shadow and Aunt Flossie's jumped up and down in the fountain. And Cock Robin propelled a languid shape whose head hung down on its chest.

'Wake up, wake up, my good shadow! Who are you? Where do you live?'

The shadow gave a loud yawn and slumped against Cock Robin. 'Mumble, mumble. Broom cupboard. Over across the Lane.'

Jane and Michael glanced at each other.

'Robertson Ay!' they said.

Round and round went the swaying shapes, hand reaching out to hand. And the children's shadows were every-where – darting after the Baby Bear or hugging the Dancing Cow.

'Really!' Mrs Corry trilled. 'I haven't had such an evening out since the days of Good Queen Bess!'

'How frivolous she is!' said her daughters, as they lumbered along together.

As for Mary Poppins, she was whirling like a spinning-top from one pair of arms to another. Now it would be the Admiral's shadow and next it would be Goosey Gander's turn. She danced a polka with Cock Robin's shadow and a

waltz with the Park Keeper's. And when the transparent
Butcher claimed her, they broke into a mad gallop, while
her own shadow stuck to her shoes and capered after her.

Twining together and interlacing, the vaporous shapes
went by. And Jane and Michael, watching the revels,
began to feel quite giddy.

'I wonder why Mary Poppins' shadow isn't free – like
the others? It's dancing beside her all the time. And so is
Mrs Corry's!' Jane turned with a frown to the Bird
Woman's shadow.

'Ah, she's cunning – that Mrs Corry! She's old and
she's learnt a lot. Let 'er shadder escape – not she! Nor
Fannie's and Annie's either. And as for Mary Poppins'
shadder –' A chuckle shook the broad shape. 'It wouldn't
leave 'er if you paid it – not for a thousand pound!'

'My turn!' cried the shadow of Old King Cole, as he
plucked Mary Poppins from the Butcher's arms and bore
her off in triumph.

'Mine, too! Mine, too!' cried a score of voices. 'Haste,
haste, no time to waste!'

Faster and faster, the music played as the fateful hour
drew nearer. The merriment was at its peak – when
suddenly, above the din, came a shrill cry of distress.

And there, at the edge of the group of dancers, stood a
small white-clad figure. It was Mrs Boom, in her dressing-
gown, with a lighted candle in her hand, looking like an
anxious hen as she gazed at the lively scene.

'Oh, please –' she pleaded. 'Will somebody help me?
The Admiral's in such a state. He's threatening to sink the
ship because he's lost his shadow. Ah, there you are!' Her
face brightened, as she spied the shape she sought. 'He's
ranting and roaring so dreadfully – won't you please come
home?'

The Admiral's shadow heaved a sigh.

'I leave him for one night in the year – and he threatens

to sink the ship! Now, that's a thing *I'd* never do. He's nothing but a spoiled child – no sense of responsibility. But I cannot disoblige you, ma'am –'

He waved his hand to his fellow-shadows and lightly blew a kiss each to Mary Poppins and Mrs Corry.

'Farewell and Adieu to you, sweet Spanish ladies!' he sang as he turned away.

'So kind of you!' chirped Mrs Boom, as she tripped beside him with her candle. 'Who's that?' she called, as they came to the Gate. 'Surely it can't be you, Miss Lark?'

A night-gowned figure was rushing through it, wrapped in a tartan shawl. And beside her, two excited dogs snatched at the trailing fringes.

'It can! It is!' Miss Lark replied, as she dashed across

the lawn. 'Oh, dear!' she moaned, as she came to the swings. 'I dreamed that my shadow had run away – and when I woke up it was true. Alas, alas, what shall I do? I can't get along without it!'

She turned her tearful eyes to the dancers and her eyebrows went up with a jerk.

'Goodgraciousme, Lucinda Emily! What are you doing here? Dancing? With strangers? In the Park? I wouldn't have thought it of you.'

'Friends – not strangers!' a voice replied, as a shadow decked in scarves and beads fluttered out of the crowd. 'I'm gayer than you think, Lucinda. And so are you, if you but knew it. Why are you always fussing and fretting instead of enjoying yourself? If you stood on your head occasionally, I'd never run away!'

'Well –' Miss Lark said doubtfully. It seemed such a strange idea.

'Come home and let's try it together!' Her shadow took her by the hand.

'I will, I will!' Miss Lark declared. And her two dogs looked at each other in horror at the thought of such a thing. 'We'll practise on the drawing-room hearthrug. Professor! What are you doing out at night? Think of your rheumatism!'

The Lane Gate opened with a creak and the Professor ambled over the grass with his hand clasped to his brow.

'Alack!' he cried. 'I've lost something. But I can't remember what it is.'

'L-look for L-lost P-property in the l-litter-b-basket!' a trembling voice advised him. The Park Keeper, dodging from bush to bush, was edging towards the dancers.

'I 'ad to come.' His teeth chattered. 'I must do my duty to the Park no matter what goes on!'

From behind the big magnolia tree he stared at the rollicking scene.

'Golly!' he muttered, reeling backwards. 'It's enough to give you the shivers! Ow! Look out! There's one of 'em comin'!'

A shadow broke away from the rest and floated towards the Professor.

'Lost something, I heard you say. And can't think what it is? Now, that's a strange coincidence – I'm in the same plight!'

It peered short-sightedly at the Professor and a sudden smile of recognition spread across its face.

'My dear fellow – can it be? *It is*. We've lost each other!'

A pair of long, transparent arms enfolded the tweed jacket. The Professor gave a crow of delight.

'Lost and found!' He embraced his shadow. 'How beautiful are those two words when one hears them both together! Oh, never let us part again! You will remember what I forget –'

'And vice versa!' his shadow cried. And the two old men wandered off with their arms around each other.

'But I tell you it's against the Rules!' The Park Keeper pulled himself together. ''Allowe'en ought to be forbidden. Get along off, you ghosts and shadows! No dancin' allowed in the Park!'

'You should talk!' jeered Mary Poppins, as she capered past with the Cat. She nodded her head towards the swings and the Park Keeper's face grew red with shame.

For there he beheld his own shadow dancing a Highland Fling!

Tee-um, tum. Tee-um, tum.
Tee-um, tee-um, tee-um.

'Stop! Whoa there! Have done!' he shouted. 'You come along with me this minute. I'm ashamed of you – breakin' the rules like this. Lumme, what's 'appenin' to me legs!'

For his feet, as though they lived a life of their own, had begun to hop and skip. Off they went – tee-um, tee-um! And by the time he had reached his shadow he, too, was doing the Highland Fling.

'Now, you keep still!' he warned it sternly, as they both slowed down together. 'Be'ave yourself like a 'uman bein'!'

'But shadows are so much nicer!' his shadow said with a giggle.

'Fred! Fred!' hissed an anxious voice, as a head in an old-fashioned nightcap came round the edge of a laurel.

'Benjamin!' the Park Keeper cried. 'What do you think you're doin'?'

'Searching for my shadow, Fred,' said the Keeper of the Zoological Gardens. 'It ran away when I wasn't looking. And I dare not face the Head Keeper unless I have it with me! A-a-ah!' He made a swoop with his net.

'Got you!' he cried, triumphantly, as he scooped up a flying shape.

His shadow gave a ghostly laugh, clear and high and tinkling.

'You've got me, Benjamin!' it trilled. 'But you haven't got my treasures. You shan't have *them* to put in a cage – they're going where they belong!'

Out of the net came an airy hand. And a cluster of tiny flitting shapes sped away through the sky. One alone fluttered over the dancers as though looking for something. Then it darted down towards the grass and settled on the left shoulder of Mary Poppins' shadow.

'A birthday gift!' piped a voice from the net, as the Keeper of the Zoological Gardens carried his shadow home.

'A butterfly for a birthday!' The friendly shadows whooped with delight.

'That's all very well,' said a cheerful voice. 'Butter-flies is all right in their place – but what about my birdies?'

Along the path came a buxom woman, with a tossing, cooing crowd of doves tumbling all about her. There was one on her hat, one on her shawl; a dove's bright eye peered out from her pocket and another from under her skirt.

'Mum!' said the Park Keeper anxiously. 'It's late for you to be out.'

Keeping a firm hold of his shadow, he hurried to her side.

'I know it, lad. But I 'ad to come. I don't so much mind about my own – but my birdies 'ave lost their shadders!'

'Excuse me, lovies!' said the Bird Woman's shadow, as she smiled at Jane and Michael. 'But I 'ave to go where I belong – that's the law, you know. Hey, old dear!' it called softly. 'Lookin' for me, I wonder?'

'I shouldn't wonder if I was!' The Bird Woman gave her shadow a calm and humorous glance. 'I got the birds, you got the shadders. And it's not for me to say which is best – but they ought to be together.'

Her shadow lightly waved its hand and the Bird Woman gave a contented chuckle. For now, beneath each grey dove, a dark shadow was flying.

'Feed the birds!' she shouted gaily.

'Tuppence a bag!' said her shadow.

'Tuppence, fourpence, sixpence, eightpence – that makes twenty-four. No, it doesn't. What's the matter? I've forgotten how to add!'

Mr Banks came slowly across the Park with his bath-robe over his shoulders. His arms were stretched out straight before him and he walked with his eyes closed.

'We're here, Daddy!' cried Jane and Michael. But Mr Banks took no notice.

'I've got my bag and the morning paper – and yet there's something missing –'

'Take him home, someone!' the shadows cried. 'He's walking in his sleep!'

And one of them – in a shadowy coat and bowler hat – sprang to Mr Banks' side.

'There, old chap! I'll do the counting. Come along back to bed.'

Mr Banks turned obediently and his sleeping face lit up.

'I thought there was something missing,' he murmured. 'But it seems I was mistaken!' He took his shadow by the arm and sauntered away with it.

'Seeking's finding – eh, ducky?' The Bird Woman nudged her shadow. 'Oh, beg pardon, Your Worship.' She bobbed a curtsey. 'I wasn't addressin' *you*!'

For the Lord Mayor and two Aldermen were advancing along the Walk. Their big cloaks billowed out behind them and their chains of office jingled.

'I 'ope I find Your Honour well?' the Bird Woman murmured politely.

'You do not, Mrs Smith,' the Lord Mayor grumbled. 'I am feeling very upset.'

'Upset, my boy?' shrieked Mrs Corry, dancing past with the Cow. 'Well, an apple a day keeps the doctor away, as I used to remind my great-great-grandson who was thrice Lord Mayor of London. Whittington, his name was. Perhaps you've heard of him?'

'Your great-great-grandfather you mean –' The Lord Mayor looked at her haughtily.

'Fiddlesticks! Indeed, I don't. Well, what's upsetting you?'

'A terrible misfortune, ma'am. I've lost –' He glanced around the Park and his eyes bulged in his head.

'That!' he cried, flinging out his hand. For there, indeed, was his portly shadow, doing its best to conceal itself behind Fannie and Annie.

'Oh, bother!' it wailed. 'What a nuisance you are! Couldn't you let me have one night off? If you knew how weary I am of processions! And as for going to see the King –'

'Certainly not!' said the Lord Mayor, 'I could never agree to appear in public without a suitable shadow. Such a suggestion is most improper and, what is more, undignified.'

'Well, you needn't be so high and mighty. You're only a Lord Mayor, you know – not the Shah of Baghdad!'

'Hic-Hic!' The Park Keeper stifled a snigger and the Lord Mayor turned to him sternly.

'Smith,' he declared, 'this is your fault. You know the rules and you break them all. Giving a party in the Park! What next, I wonder? I'm afraid there's nothing for it, Smith, but to speak to the Lord High Chancellor!'

'It's not *my* party, Yer Worship – please! Give me another chance, Yer Honour. Think of me pore old –'

'Don't you worry about me, Fred!' The Bird Woman snapped her fingers sharply.

And at once the doves clapped their wings and swooped towards the Lord Mayor. They sat on his head, they sat

on his nose, they tucked their tail-feathers down his neck and fluttered inside his cloak.

'Oh, don't! I'm a ticklish man! Hee, hee!' The Lord Mayor, quite against his will, burst into helpless laughter.

'Remove these birds at once, Smith! I won't be tickled – oh, ha, ha!'

He laughed, he crowed, he guffawed, he tittered, ducking and whirling among the dancers as he tried to escape the doves.

'Not under my chin! – Oh, oh! – Have mercy! Oof! There's one inside my sleeve. Oh, ha, ha, ha, ha, ha, ha, hee! Dear me! Is that you, Miss Mary Poppins? Well, that makes all the – tee-hee! – difference. You're so re – ho, ho! – spectable.' The Lord Mayor writhed as the soft feathers rustled behind his ears.

'What a wonderful party you're having!' he shrieked. 'Ha, ha! Ho, ho! I should have come sooner. Listen! I hear my favourite tune – "Over the hills and far away!" Hee, hee! Ha, ha! And far away!'

'Is there anything the matter, your honour?' The Policeman, with Ellen on his arm, strode towards the revels.

'There is!' The Lord Mayor giggled wildly. 'I'm ticklish and I can't stop laughing. Everything seems so terribly funny – and you in particular. Do you realize you've lost your shadow? It's over there on a swing – hee, hee! – playing a concertina!'

'No shadow, sir? A concertina?' The Policeman gaped at the Lord Mayor as though he had lost his wits. 'Nobody's got a shadow, your honour. And shadows don't play on concertinas – at least, not to my knowledge.'

'Don't be so – tee-hee! – silly, man. Everyone's got a shadow!'

'Not at this moment they haven't, your worship! There's a cloud coming over the moon!'

'Alas! A cloud! It came too soon! When shall we meet again?'

A shadowy wailing filled the air. For even as the Policeman spoke, the bright moon veiled her face. Darkness dropped like a cloak on the scene and before the eyes of the watching children every shadow vanished. The merry music died away. And as silence fell upon the Park the steeples above the sleeping city rang their midnight chime.

'Our time is up!' cried the plaintive voices. 'Hallowe'en's over! Away, away!'

Light as a breeze, past Jane and Michael, the invisible shadows swept.

'Farewell!' said one.

'Adieu!' another.

And a third at the edge of Jane's ear piped a note on his flute.

'Feed the birds, tuppence a bag!' The Bird Woman whistled softly. And the doves crept out of the Lord Mayor's sleeve and from under the brim of his hat.

Nine! Ten! Eleven! Twelve! The bells of midnight ceased.

'Farewell! Farewell!' called the fading voices.

'Over the hills and far away!' came the far-off fluting echo.

'Oh, Tom, the Piper's Son,' cried Jane. 'When shall we see you again?'

Then something softer than air touched them, enfolded them and drew them away.

'Who are you?' they cried in the falling night. They seemed to be floating on wings of darkness, over the Park and home.

And the answer came from without and within them.

'Your other selves – your shadows . . .'

*

'Hrrrrrumph!' The Lord Mayor gave himself a shake as though he were coming out of a dream.

'Farewell!' he murmured, waving his hand. 'Though who – or what – I'm saying it to, I really do not know. I seemed to be part of a beautiful party. All so merry! But where have they gone?'

'I expect you're over-tired, your worship!' The Police-man, closely followed by Ellen, drew him away to the Long Walk and the gate that led to the City.

Behind them marched the Aldermen, solemn and dis-approving.

'I expect I am,' the Lord Mayor said. 'But it didn't *feel* like that . . .'

The Park Keeper glanced around the Park and took his mother's arm. Darkness filled the sky like a tide. In all the world, as far as his watchful eyes could see, there were only two points of light.

'That there star,' he said, pointing, 'and the night-light in Number Seventeen – if you look at 'em long enough, mum, you can 'ardly tell which is which!'

The Bird Woman drew her doves about her and smiled at him comfortably.

'Well, one's the shadder of the other! Let's be goin', lad . . .'

Michael came slowly in to breakfast, looking back over his shoulder. And slowly, slowly, a dark shape followed him over the floor.

'My shadow's here – is yours, Jane?'

'Yes,' she said, sipping her milk. She had been awake a long time, smiling at her shadow. And it seemed to her, as the sun shone in, that her shadow was smiling back.

'And where else would they be, pray? Take your por-ridge, please.'

Mary Poppins, in a fresh white apron, crackled into the room. She was carrying her best blue coat and the hat with the crimson tulip.

'Well – sometimes they're in the Park,' said Jane. She gave the white apron a cautious glance. What would it say to *that*? she wondered.

The coat went on to its hook with a jerk and the hat seemed to leap to its paper bag.

'In the Park – or the garden – or up a tree! A shadow goes wherever you go. Don't be silly, Jane.'

'But sometimes they escape, Mary Poppins.' Michael reached for the sugar. 'Like ours, last night, at the Hallowe'en Party!'

'Hallowe'en Party?' she said, staring. And you would have thought, to look at her, she had never heard those words before.

'Yes,' he said rashly, taking no notice. 'But your shadow never runs away – does it, Mary Poppins?'

She glanced across at the nursery mirror and met her own reflection. The blue eyes glowed, the pink cheeks shone and the mouth wore a small, complacent smile.

'Why should it want to?' she said, sniffing. Run away? The idea!

'Not for a thousand pounds!' cried Michael. And the memory of the night's adventure bubbled up inside him. 'Oh, how I laughed at the Lord Mayor!' He spluttered at the very thought. 'And Mrs Corry! And Goosey Gander!'

'And you, Mary Poppins,' giggled Jane. 'Hopping about all over the Park – and the butterfly on your shadow's shoulder!'

Michael and Jane looked at each other and roared with mirth. They flung back their heads and held their sides and rolled around in their chairs.

'Oh, dear! I'm choking! How funny it was!'

'Indeed?'

A voice as sharp as an icicle brought them up with a jerk.

They stopped in the middle of a laugh and tried to compose their faces. For the bright blue eyes of Mary Poppins were wide with shocked surprise.

'Hopping about? With a butterfly? At night? In a public place? Do you sit there, Jane and Michael Banks, and call me a kangaroo?'

This, they could see, was the last straw. The camel's back was broken.

'Sitting on Goosey Gander's shoulder? Hopping and flying all over the Park – is that what you're trying to tell me?'

'Well, not like a kangaroo, Mary Poppins. But you *were* hopping, I *think* –' Michael plunged for the right word as she glared at him over the teapot. But the sight of her face was too much for him. Out of the corner of his eye he looked across at Jane.

'Help me!' he cried to her silently. 'Surely we did not dream it?'

But Jane, from the corner of *her* eye, was looking back at him. 'No, it was true!' she seemed to say. For she gave her head a little shake and pointed towards the floor.

Michael looked down.

There lay Mary Poppins' shadow, neatly spread out upon the carpet. Jane's shadow and his own were leaning up against it, and upon its shoulder, black in the sun, was a shadowy butterfly.

'Oh!' cried Michael joyfully, dropping his spoon with a clatter.

'Oh, what?' said Mary Poppins tartly, glancing down at the floor.

She looked from the butterfly to Michael and then from Michael to Jane. And the porridge grew cold on their three plates as they all gazed at each other. Nothing was said – there was nothing to say. There were things, they knew, that could not be told. And, anyway, what did it matter? The three linked shadows on the floor understood it all.

'It's your birthday, isn't it, Mary Poppins?' said Michael at last, with a grin.

'Many happy returns, Mary Poppins!' Jane gave her hand a pat.

A pleased smile crept about her mouth, but she pursed her lips to prevent it.

'Who told you that?' she inquired, sniffing. As if she didn't know!

But Michael was full of joy and courage. If Mary Poppins never explained, why, indeed, should he? He only shook his head and smiled.

'I wonder!' he said, in a priggish voice exactly like her own.

'Impudence!' She sprang at him. But he darted, laughing, away from the table, out of the nursery and down the stairs, with Jane close at his heels.

Along the garden path they ran, through the gate and over the Lane and into the waiting Park.

The morning air was bright and clear, the birds were singing their autumn songs, and the Park Keeper was coming towards them with a late rose stuck in his cap . . .

Chelsea, London
March 1952

G. I. E. D.

P. L. Travers was born in Australia of Irish and Scottish stock and has spent most of her time in England and Ireland. All her life, her great love has been myth, legend and fairy-tale, so it is not surprising that first *Mary Poppins* and then *Friend Monkey*, solid and down-to-earth as they are, seem to be lit from within by this love. If you ask her how she came to write these books she will say that she doesn't know.

And if you ask what is the best thing that ever happened to her she will say, 'Oh, the roses!' Wheatcroft have developed a beautiful, large-hearted yellow and golden rose called *Mary Poppins* and a horticulturist in the United States has made a pink *Mary Poppins*, a *Sleeping Beauty* (because it is P. L. Travers' favourite fairy-tale) and a deep pink *Pamela Travers*.

Other Puffins by P. L. Travers

A DOG CALLED NELSON

Bill Naughton

Nelson is a remarkable one-eyed mongrel who lives with a large and chaotic family in the bottom end house of Bill's street in Lancashire. Despite being one-eyed, Nelson is busier than most ordinary dogs. Whether it is the weekly picture show, a joke-telling session or a game of football, Nelson will be there, or even if he isn't, he's one of those dogs that has a way of getting into your thoughts . . .

SUMMER SWITCH

Mary Rodgers

It had all happened in a flash. One moment Ben's father was himself – the next he wasn't. He had swapped bodies with his twelve-year-old son, who didn't seem too keen to swap back! An amazing adventure, bursting with humour, from the author of *Freaky Friday*.

MAGNUS POWERMOUSE
Dick King-Smith

Magnus was a large mouse, a fearless mouse, a real power-mouse! His mother was amazed when she saw the size of her newborn infant and realized that feeding him was going to cause problems. Small wonder that she turned to a box of patent Porker Pills, used for fattening pigs, in order to feed her voracious offspring. Small wonder, too, that Magnus just grew – and the bigger he grew, the more problems he caused.

SUPER GRAN IS MAGIC
Forrest Wilson

Super Gran wasn't all that bothered about Mr Black's new invention: a small black box that could hypnotize people and animals. But then a rotten stage magician called Mystico thought of the perfect way to make his act more exciting: he'd set a hypnotized Super Gran to work for him. So suddenly Super Gran had to call on all her Super-powers! Another comic adventure featuring everyone's favourite senior citizen.